She folded the paper in half, her vision blurring with tears. Her neighbor's visit had shaken her to the core.

When she'd heard the deep rumble of a man's voice, she'd panicked. She turned off the shower and leapt out of the stall in a surge of adrenaline. Wrapping a towel around her body, she burst from the bathroom and rushed down the hall.

Seeing a strange man inside her house had brought back terrible memories. Eighteen months ago, she'd walked in on her husband's murderer. She'd dropped her groceries and run out of the house, calling 911 on her cell phone.

The criminal was still at large—and Leah prayed he'd never find her.

Her neighbor looked nothing like the cold villain who'd shot John in the head. He was taller, leaner, not quite as dark. As soon as he introduced himself, she recognized him as the surfer next door. She saw the man coming back from the beach almost every morning. He was always barefoot, surfboard under one arm, wet suit pulled down to the waist. Something about him made her uncomfortable.

Unsettled by the surprise encounter, she peeked through the horizontal blinds, studying her neighbor's driveway. He'd moved in about a month ago. His beat-up white truck said Cosgrove Construction on the passenger side. His house was small and rundown; she was surprised it hadn't been razed.

He was just another down-on-his-luck handyman.

She let the blinds snap shut, aware that she'd overreacted and embarrassed him. She'd also yelled at the girls in front of him, which made her feel lousy. Mandy, in particular, was sensitive to loud voices. Alyssa was too young to remember the fights.

After she secured the lock on the front door, Leah went to her bedroom and pulled on her bathrobe. In her manic state, she hadn't even thought about donning it. She must have looked like a crazy woman.

She'd also forgotten to set the security alarm before she hopped in the shower. An unforgivable oversight.

Shaking her head, she padded to the girls' room. Mandy had slammed the door shut, which wasn't allowed but she let it pass, turning the knob and slipping inside. The space was cramped, filled with two single beds. Alyssa was playing with an ABC puzzle on the floor. Mandy lay on her bed, arms crossed over her chest.

She was mad. Well, so was Leah.

Knotting the belt at her waist, she sat down on Alyssa's bed, addressing both daughters. "What have I told you about opening the door to strangers?"

"Not to do it," Alyssa answered promptly.

"So why did you?"

Mandy stared up at the ceiling, petulant.

"It wasn't a stranger," Alyssa pointed out. "It was Santa."

"It wasn't Santa, dummy," Mandy said.

"Hey," Leah scolded. "Be nice."

"Who was it?" Alyssa asked.

"A man pretending to be Santa," Leah said.

"Was he a bad man?"

"Probably not, but you girls need to be more careful. I don't want anyone to hurt you or take you away from me."

Hearing the quiver in Leah's voice, Alyssa looked up from her puzzle. She scrambled to her feet and gave Leah a hug. "Okay, Mommy. I love you."

Leah pressed her lips to the top of Alyssa's head. "I love you, too, sweetie."

Mandy let out an exaggerated sigh. She pretended not to like displays of affection. When Alyssa let go, Leah leaned over Mandy, kissing her nose before she could squirm away. "I'm counting on you to watch over your sister."

Mandy's expression softened. She was already protective of Alyssa, and enjoyed being responsible. "He wasn't bad, Mom."

"How do you know? Because he had presents?"

"He liked your cookies."

"That doesn't mean anything," she said, her cheeks heating. If she wasn't mistaken, she'd also seen a hint of masculine appreciation in his gaze. Brian Cosgrove liked full-grown women. And he knew a good cookie when he tasted one. She felt guilty for throwing him out of her house.

Taking a deep breath, she removed the Dear Santa letter from her front pocket. "Why did you put this in his mailbox?"

"I didn't want you to see it before the mailman came."

She looked from one daughter to the other, pressure building behind her eyes. "You know that your daddy isn't coming back, right?"

Alyssa's face fell. She nodded once and returned to her floor puzzle. Mandy focused on the ceiling, her chin quivering. This was a subject they'd all rather avoid. John hadn't been a perfect husband or an ideal father, but they missed him.

On days like this, the loss was almost unbearable.

Leah couldn't scold them for writing the letter, or for wanting their father back. She felt powerless over the situation. If only John had been able to control his gambling addiction. If only Leah had discovered his secret earlier.

Pushing aside her regrets, she rose from the bed and went back to her room to get ready. She had to apologize to Brian. Her stomach tightened at the prospect and she nibbled on the edge of her fingernail, wondering what to wear. She'd planned to spend the day toiling in the kitchen. The choices were limited because she owned few nice outfits. After rifling through her clothes, she put on her best jeans and a dark green tank top.

Vanity had her reaching for the makeup kit in the back of her underwear drawer. She applied a touch of mascara and a hint of lip gloss, her hands trembling. After shoving her feet into black flats and running a brush through her damp, shoulder-length hair, she walked down the hall to retrieve the presents.

Brian had bought her daughters exactly what they'd asked for. The toys were from two different stores, and had probably cost him a day's hard labor. She took the half-wrapped gifts to the girls' bedroom, watching their eyes brighten with hope. "I'm going next door to say sorry. You both stay right here."

"Can we play with our new toys?"

"I suppose," she said, setting them down. If Brian didn't accept her apology, she'd offer to pay him back for the gifts.

"Thanks, Mommy!"

"We'll have to write a thank-you note."

They both agreed, tearing into their presents. Leah never left them unsupervised but she'd only be gone a minute. Tugging on the hem of her shirt, she walked outside, squinting at the strong California sunshine.

In Kansas City, they'd have had a white Christmas.

Her pulse fluttered as she approached his screen door. The thin barrier was torn in several places, and had a flimsy-looking frame. If she wanted to, she could slip her hand inside and reach the latch. She felt a twinge of resentment over his lackadaisical security. Single women couldn't afford to be so careless.

As she raised her hand to knock, she saw Brian standing in the kitchen. He'd ditched the fur-trimmed coat and not bothered to put on a shirt. His skin was smooth and tanned, his torso etched with muscle.

While she watched, her mouth going dry, he lifted a plastic water bottle to his lips and took a long drink. Her eyes traveled from his strong brown throat, which worked as he swallowed, to the fine sheen of perspiration on his chest. The red Santa pants he was wearing rode dangerously low on his waist, held up by a thin white drawstring, and his stomach looked as flat and tight as a drum. This was no bowl full of jelly.

She might have made a noise, because he caught sight of her and startled, the bottle slipping from his hand. It bounced off the tile floor, spilling everywhere.

"Damn!"

"I'm sorry," Leah said, clapping a hand over her eyes. Maybe if she didn't stare at his naked chest, she could remember what she'd walked over here for.

He scrambled around for a minute, sopping up the water with paper towels. As he came toward the door, still shirtless, she tried to keep her gaze above his neck. It was a difficult task because he was a head taller than her.

"I'm sorry," she said again, making no move to step inside when he opened the door. From what she could see, there was no furniture. A table saw with a long, orange extension cord dominated the living room. "I just wanted to apologize for being so rude. My girls aren't supposed to open the door to strangers."

He leaned against the screen, holding it ajar. "I didn't think of that."

"Well, you're not a mother."

The corner of his mouth tipped up. "True."

She moistened her lips, flustered. "It was really nice of you to bring the gifts." Before he had a chance to reply, she rushed ahead. "Look, it's Christmas, and we have plenty of food. Would you like to join us for dinner?"

His brows rose in surprise.

"I mean, I'm sure you have other plans." She glanced into the empty space behind him. "But if not, we'd be happy to have you."

He hesitated. "Actually, I don't have other plans."

They stared at each other for a long moment. "Well, great," she said, forcing a smile. "Everything should be ready at noon."

"You eat dinner at noon?"

Leah remembered that Californians didn't use the same terms as Midwesterners. "Lunch, I should say."

He gave her a curious look. "What's your name?"

"Leah," she said, careful not to add the *n*. Back in Kansas, she'd been Leanne. Now she was just Leah. Her identity, her family, her entire world—slashed.

"Pleased to meet you," he said, sticking out his hand.

She shook it quickly, noting that his palm felt warm and hard and as tough as leather. "See you at noon?"

He nodded. "I'll be there."

Smile faltering, she backed away, almost tripping over an uneven place in the sidewalk. He really needed to get that fixed.

Chapter 2

Leah made a traditional Christmas meal.

There was spiral ham, scalloped potatoes and fresh green beans. She'd steamed corn on the cob and made rolls from scratch. If anyone had room for dessert, she'd offer a warm cherry torte with vanilla ice cream.

Brian arrived on time, but Leah wasn't quite ready. Mandy and Alyssa had been in high spirits all morning, running wild through the house. They tended to get overexcited on holidays, especially when Leah was too busy to discipline them. After she got fed up, threatening to take their presents away, they sat down to write Brian a thank-you note.

At the sound of the doorbell, she wiped her hands on a towel and went to answer it, glancing through the peephole. Her neighbor had cleaned up a little. His hair was combed back, his face freshly shaved. He'd also brought another gift—a large poinsettia.

Smoothing her apron, she opened the door. "Hi."

"Hi."

She waved him in, studying his appearance from beneath lowered lashes. He was older than she'd first estimated, at least thirty. Years of surfing or working outdoors had given him a rugged, weathered look. His T-shirt and jeans were far from new, but his boots were spotless and he smelled good. Like soap and sawdust.

She locked the door behind him, gesturing at the poinsettia. "You didn't have to bring anything."

"It was no trouble."

"Well, thank you," she said, accepting the gift. Their fingertips brushed as he transferred the plant to her. Heart jittering, she stuck the poinsettia on the coffee table, admiring its festive red leaves.

He nodded hello to the girls, who regarded him with curiosity. "I'm Brian," he said. "You might remember me as Santa."

"This is Mandy," Leah said, touching her older daughter's head, "and that's Alyssa."

"Pleased to meet you both."

The girls shed their shyness like a winter coat. "I drew you a picture!" Alyssa said, hopping to her feet. She showed him a drawing of a stick figure in a red hat and coat, standing next to a colorful green triangle. Not to be outdone, Mandy brandished her own artwork, a thank-you note decorated with bows and boxes. "I made you a *card*."

Brian weighed the merits of each offering, giving them equal attention. "I like the Christmas tree," he said to Alyssa, who beamed at the praise. Smiling, he turned to Mandy. "And you write very well for a first-grader."

"I'm in kindergarten," she said.

"Really? You must be the smartest girl in class."

She glanced sideways at Leah, her face solemn. Mandy wasn't as good a reader as Brittany, one of the other students. But she tried very hard at school and Leah couldn't have been more proud of her. "I'm not."

He chuckled at her honesty. "What about you?" he asked Alyssa.

"I'm the best drawer," she said, ever-humble.

"I can see that."

"Why don't you girls set the table?" Leah suggested.

While Mandy transferred the good plates from the hutch, Alyssa dispersed the silverware, and Leah walked to the kitchen to take the rolls out of the oven. It was a warm day, even by California standards, and she was sweating. Shifting the rolls into a basket, she pushed a lock of hair off her forehead.

"Can I do anything to help?" Brian asked.

"Yes," she said, taking the basket to the table. "We need drinks." She'd already set out cups of water for the girls. "Do you like iced tea?"

"Sure."

"There's a pitcher in the fridge, and glasses in the cabinet."

He found the iced tea and poured them each a tall glass, following her as she moved the serving dishes to the table. Alyssa had given herself two spoons, so Leah switched one with Mandy, nodding her approval. "Let's eat."

She'd planned to sit at the head of the table, but Brian took that chair. Although it felt odd to see another man in John's place, asking him to move would be impolite. Leah glanced at the pronged fork near his right hand, aware that it could be used as a weapon.

He seemed to notice her discomfort. "Is this okay?"

"Of course," she said, as if nothing was amiss. Instead of sitting down, she stood beside Brian and picked up the sharp fork, spearing a juicy section of ham. She served him first, because he was a guest. Then she dispersed slices of ham to the girls and herself. Bringing the fork to the opposite end of the table with her, she sat down.

The side dishes were passed around next, and with slightly less trepidation. Alyssa expressed her hatred for all vegetables and Mandy dropped a dinner roll, but that was par for the course. Leah put her napkin in her lap and reminded the girls to do the same, noting that Brian mimicked them. He also waited for Leah's cue to start eating.

She felt self-conscious about not trusting him with the pronged fork. Instead of making stilted conversation, she tucked into her plate, pleased when Brian did the same. Unlike her daughters, who were picky eaters, he appeared to appreciate a home-cooked meal. Leah had forgotten how satisfying it felt to watch someone enjoy her food.

When the girls were finished, they started fidgeting and kicking their legs under the table. "Can we have ice cream?"

"In a few minutes," she said, noting that they'd both eaten a fair amount. She rarely insisted that they clean their plates. "Wash up and go play."

They took their dishes to the sink and ran off, eager to get back to their Christmas fun. Leah hadn't been able to afford many gifts this year, but the Witness Protection Program had come through with some toys and art supplies. Along with the inexpensive items she'd purchased, and Santa's surprise gifts, they had plenty to occupy them.

Brian ate every morsel on his plate, his fork scraping the flat surface.

"Would you like another helping?" Leah asked, amused.

He deliberated, obviously wanting more. She didn't know where he'd put it on that lean frame.

"Go ahead," she said with a smile, taking her own plate to the sink. "There's plenty." While she rinsed some dishes and tidied up the kitchen, he polished off a second serving of everything. "How is it?"

"Delicious. I think this is the best food I've ever eaten."

Her cheeks heated at the compliment, which sounded sincere. She left the ice cream to thaw on the countertop and brought the cherry torte to the table, wondering how long it had been since he'd had a decent meal.

"I've been living on convenience store burritos."

"That explains it," she said, taking her seat.

He wiped his mouth with the napkin, shaking his head. "No, this is something special. Are you a chef?"

Before the girls came along, she'd gone to culinary school. "I decorate ice cream cakes in a warehouse," she said, rolling her eyes, "but I've always loved to cook." Her current job was a waste of her creative talents. Maybe in a few years she'd be placed somewhere more fitting. "What kind of construction work do you do?"

"Any kind. I specialize in custom carpentry, but I have a general contractor's license, so I can take whatever's available." He leaned back in his chair, his expression sardonic. "Sometimes I dig ditches."

Leah admired his good-natured attitude. Here she was, feeling sorry for herself because cake-decorating wasn't a challenge. At least she didn't have to dig trenches and lay bricks or whatever else he did. This poor guy had no furniture, no appliances. But he'd been kind enough to buy Christmas gifts for his neighbors.

"I know those presents were expensive," she said. "Would you be offended if I offered to pay you back?"

His eyes darkened. "Yes."

She drank another sip of tea, feeling awkward. Although he seemed nice, she didn't know anything about him. She wanted to ask why he'd decided to play Santa, why he was alone on Christmas, and if he had a family of his own.

"I have two nieces," he said, as if reading her mind. "Twins."

Leah warmed to the subject. "Twins? How old are they?"

"Almost four. I bought the Santa suit two years ago, with them in mind."

"How did they like it?"

A creased formed between his brows. "They never saw it. My sister…their mother…died in a car accident that year."

She lifted a hand to her lips. "Oh, my God. I'm so sorry."

He inclined his head. "Her husband was from the East Coast, so he moved back there with my nieces a few months later."

"Have you seen them since?"

"No. He's remarried and…they don't remember me. I don't think they remember *her*."

"Oh, my God," she repeated, stunned. "That's awful."

He didn't disagree.

She struggled to think of something comforting to say. "Alyssa was a baby when her father died, so it's been easier for her. Mandy took it hard. I try not to dwell on the loss, but I can't imagine pretending he didn't exist."

"You still talk about him?"

"Maybe not as much as I should," she admitted, seeing her neighbor in a different light. When he'd read Mandy and Alyssa's letter, he must have been reminded of his nieces. It was a tragic situation. "I'm so sorry I threw you out earlier. I didn't realize."

"It's okay," he replied, relaxing a little. "I'm only telling you this because I don't want you to get the wrong idea about…what kind of person I am." His gaze fell to the pronged fork on the table, out of his reach.

"I'm overprotective," she said, chagrined. "I don't mean any insult."

He gave her a curious look, as if contemplating the reason for her caution.

The girls burst back on the scene, begging for dessert, so Leah rose to get the ice cream. Grabbing a few small plates, she scooped smooth vanilla bean alongside the warm cherry torte. "Do you want some?" she asked Brian, serving her daughters first this time.

"Is it as good as the cookies?"

"Better," she said.

His brows rose in agreement as he took a first bite. "Wow."

Leah lifted a spoon to her mouth, enjoying the sweet, tart cherries and creamy vanilla ice cream. By the time dessert was over, they were all stuffed. Mandy and Alyssa had both been up since the crack of dawn and looked tired. Leah put on a Disney movie for them and returned to the kitchen, surprised to see Brian at the sink.

"I thought I'd help you load the dishwasher."

"It doesn't work," she said, surprised. "I've never used it."

"Do you mind if I take a look?"

"Go ahead."

He glanced into the cabinet under the sink, checking the wiring. "It's not hooked up right."

"Really?"

"I can fix it if you want."

She crossed her arms over her chest, drumming her fingertips against her elbows. "How long will it take?"

"Half an hour."

"What do you charge?"

He shrugged. "A plate of leftovers."

"I was going to offer you that anyway."

"Then it's a deal. I'll get my tools."

Brian came back five minutes later with a scarred metal toolbox. Setting it on the floor, he opened the sink cabinet and hunkered down. "You have an old towel?"

She had nothing *but* old towels. Grabbing a couple of different sizes from the bathroom, she brought them to him. He placed one of the large ones over the lip of the cabinet, making a more comfortable spot to lean against. Then he stretched out on his back and got to work, unscrewing bolts and taking the plumbing apart.

With his head under the sink and his long legs sticking out, he should have looked odd. Instead he seemed at ease, even masterful. There was something very manly about this task. As he cranked a wrench, shifting his weight in the cramped space, the hem of his T-shirt rode up, revealing a strip of his taut abdomen. She averted her gaze.

John had never been handy with tools.

Leah concentrated on putting away the leftovers. She packed a hefty portion of ham, potatoes, and green beans into a plastic container for Brian. Then she wrapped a piece of cherry torte in foil and added a tin of cookies to the stash.

"There," he said, making a final adjustment. "Turn it on."

She pressed the button to start the dishwasher. Water rushed into the machine, beginning a new cycle. "It works!"

He moved his head out from underneath the sink. "Run it once without any dishes to make sure."

"Thank you so much," she said, marveling at his skills. She'd been meaning to get the dishwasher fixed for ages. "You're a lifesaver."

"It was nothing."

"Are you sure I can't pay you?"

He gathered up his tools, preparing to leave. "I'm sure."

Leah was both sorry and relieved to see him go. Although she enjoyed his company and appreciated his help, his presence unnerved her in a way she didn't want to analyze. She also couldn't afford to let anyone get too close. Intuition told her that Brian Cosgrove had a canny mind, along with deft hands.

To keep her children safe, she had to stay guarded.

Turning back to the counter, she put the food containers in a striped gift bag. "Merry Christmas," she said, handing it to him.

He accepted the bag with a polite nod and she saw him out, locking the door behind him. As soon as he was gone, the house seemed empty. And too quiet. She went to check on the girls, noting that Alyssa had fallen asleep with Dr. Elmo in her arms. Mandy was still watching *101 Dalmations*.

Leah curled up beside her, staring sightlessly at the screen.

* * *

Brian wasn't able to relax when he came home from Leah's.

The meal had been fantastic. Even after tasting her cookies, he hadn't expected her to be such a good cook. Maybe because she was on the slender side and had kind of a skittish personality. Sharing a meal with a neighbor seemed out of character for her. Brian imagined that most chefs were round and gregarious.

It wasn't that she wasn't friendly. It was more like she wasn't *happy.*

She'd lost her husband and was raising two kids on her own, so that was understandable. Most women in her position wouldn't feel overjoyed.

But there was a deeper issue with her, he suspected. She'd panicked when she saw him this morning. She'd also made sure he didn't have access to the serving fork. Although his sister had often moved sharp items out of the children's reach, Leah's kids weren't babies. She considered him a threat.

He wasn't insulted by her attitude. She was a protective mother and he respected that. What unsettled him was the thought of someone traumatizing her so badly that she expected others to do the same.

In a way, she reminded him of himself. He'd been bounced around a lot when he was a kid. So had his little sister. A few of the foster homes they'd lived in were just as dysfunctional as his mother's house, and it wasn't unusual for him to get picked on or roughed up. As he got older he'd become less of a target. He'd learned how to defend himself and his sister, but he'd never forgotten how it felt to be small and scared.

During the meal, he'd wondered if Leah's husband

had been abusive. Then her eyes had softened when she spoke of him and he dismissed the idea.

Whatever she'd gone through was none of his business. He was drawn to her and he had the strange feeling that she shared his interest. But he also realized that she didn't welcome the attraction. He should forget about their impromptu Christmas get-together.

She wouldn't invite him back.

Brian decided to keep an eye out for her anyway. The remodel would take several more months, and he liked the idea of being her unofficial security guard. No one could approach Leah's house without him noticing.

He'd had no control over his foster-care childhood or his sister's untimely death. He had no chance at having a relationship with his nieces, his only relatives. But he could take on the responsibility of watching over Leah and her children.

He could do it from a distance.

Chapter 3

Leanne was driving home from the grocery store, humming along to the radio.

Baby Melissa was fast asleep in her car seat. Leanne parked in the driveway and grabbed several bags of groceries, walking inside. John's car had been alone in the garage, so she was surprised to hear more than one voice coming from the bedroom. Her husband sounded desperate, the other man, angry.

Frowning, she went down the hall. An intense wave of foreboding washed over her, and she almost turned around to go back to the car. Instinct told her to get Melissa and run. Instead, she moved quietly, softening her steps.

The door was cracked open. As she peered inside, her blood turned to ice. John knelt on the carpet, pleading for mercy. The man standing over him showed none. While she watched, he pulled out a gun and shot her husband in the head.

Leanne was too terrified to scream. But John's killer looked up and their eyes locked. It was Mariano Felix, one of his "business associates."

She dropped the groceries in the hall and fled. She ran through the garage, past the driveway, across the yard. She left her car. There was no time to put the keys in the ignition, and she didn't want to endanger her daughter.

Heart pounding, she sailed over the hedge, into the neighbor's yard, and ducked down out of sight. Her purse was still hanging off her shoulder. With a shaking hand, she reached for her cell phone, dialing 911.

Heart hammering, she peeked over the hedge. Felix burst from the house, approaching the driver's-side door of her car.

"No!" she screamed.

He turned his head, catching sight of her behind the hedge.

She straightened, showing him the cell phone. An emergency operator had already responded to her call. "Please," she said, begging for help. Begging for her life. For her baby's life.

The neighborhood was quiet, but it wasn't deserted. There were people in the nearby houses, cars on the street. Felix took off at a brisk pace, choosing not to murder her in front of dozens of possible witnesses.

He rounded the corner and disappeared.

She woke up in a cold sweat, his cruel face etched in her memory. The police had never found the loan shark who'd killed her husband. He was a cold-blooded criminal in a mafia organization and a very real threat to her.

The nightmare came less frequently now, over a year later. But it still had the power to set her nerves on edge.

Rising from the bed, she changed clothes, donning a pair of jean shorts and a white tank top. Judging by the

Praise for
Jill Sorenson

"With Jill Sorenson, you are guaranteed a dangerously addictive, gut-wrenchingly tight-paced read."
—*New York Times* bestselling author Stephanie Tyler

"Sorenson's sleek sensuality and fresh new voice are sure to score big with readers."
—*New York Times* bestselling author Cindy Gerard

"This heartwarming adventure story has an unusual setting and perfect details, making it one of the best books of the year."

—*RT Book Reviews* on *Stranded with Her Ex*
(4.5 stars, Top Pick)

"*Buy this book. I LOVED it.*"
—*New York Times* and *USA TODAY* bestselling author Maya Banks on *Tempted by Her Target*

Praise for
Jennifer Morey

"Great characterization and a thrilling plot make this a must-read book."
— *RT Book Reviews* on *Special Ops Affair*

"The story starts with strong emotion and the action is fast throughout.... This is a heartwarming book."
—*RT Book Reviews* on *The Librarian's Secret Scandal*

"Morey is an experienced writer who easily picks up the threads of the Colton family with imaginative and fairly true-to-life characters."
—*TheRomanceReader.com* on *The Librarian's Secret Scandal*

JILL SORENSON

writes sexy romantic suspense for Harlequin Books and Bantam. Her books have appeared in *Cosmopolitan* magazine.

After earning a degree in literature and a bilingual teaching credential from California State University, she decided teaching wasn't her cup of tea. She started writing one day while her firstborn was taking a nap and hasn't stopped since. She lives in San Diego with her husband and two young daughters.

JENNIFER MOREY

A two-time 2009 RITA®-Award nominee and a Golden Quill winner for Best First Book for *The Secret Soldier,* Jennifer Morey writes contemporary romance and romantic suspense. Project manager du jour, she works for the space systems segment of a satellite imagery and information company and lives in sunny Denver, Colorado. She can be reached through her website, www.jennifermorey.com, and on Facebook—jmorey2009@gmail.com.

JILL SORENSON

JENNIFER MOREY

Risky Christmas

ROMANTIC
SUSPENSE

ISBN-13: 978-0-373-27749-0

RISKY CHRISTMAS

Recycling programs
for this product may
not exist in your area.

Printed in U.S.A.

CONTENTS

Dear Reader,

Ah, November. Where has the year gone? Whatever the answer, you can stop time with the latest adrenaline-pumping romances from Harlequin Romantic Suspense Books!

Be sure to start your holiday season with Jill Sorenson's and Jennifer Morey's fun, sexy stories in our yuletide 2-in-1 entitled *Risky Christmas* (#1679). One lonely widow finds love—and danger—in hiding, while an excitement-starved heroine gets what she wishes for in a thrill ride with a rugged FBI agent. Don't miss these wonderful tales! Elle Kennedy contributes to our popular miniseries The Kelley Legacy with a harrowing rescue of a high-profile pregnant senator's daughter in *Missing Mother-To-Be* (#1680).

Don't miss reader favorite Carla Cassidy's *Cowboy's Triplet Trouble* (#1681), which is part of our baby-themed series, Top Secret Deliveries. Here, a single mom goes to confront the father of her three babies and falls for—wait for it—the man's triplet brother! In Gail Barrett's *High-Risk Reunion* (#1682), part of a new miniseries called Stealth Knights, a professional thief runs into his ex on a secret mission, and they end up framed for murder!

As always, we'll deliver on our promise of breathtaking romance set against a backdrop of suspense. Have a wonderful November and happy reading!

Sincerely,

Patience Bloom

Senior Editor

HOLIDAY SECRETS

Jill Sorenson

For my daughters

Chapter 1

Brian adjusted the red stocking cap, trying to cover his dark brown hair.

He'd bought the costume on a whim a few years ago with the intention to play Santa for his sister's children. Due to unfortunate circumstances, it had never been used. The cheap red suit came with an itchy white beard, but no wig. His own black rubber boots, which he used to wade through concrete, completed the look.

Leaving the hat askew, he stepped back and studied his reflection. He needed a haircut. His costume was "one size fits all" and poorly made. The fuzzy white cuffs of the jacket didn't reach his wrists, the pants were too baggy, and the black plastic belt gaped at his waist. He looked like Homeless Santa.

He grabbed a pillow from the mattress on the floor and stuffed it under his jacket, fashioning a jolly paunch. There, that was better. As he headed outside, he picked up the bag of gifts and put the Dear Santa letter in his front pocket.

At 9:00 a.m., the sun was already blazing. It was going to be a hot Christmas in Oceanside, California. There wasn't a cloud in the perfect blue sky. Brian had spent most of the morning on his surfboard, and the waves were in fine form. He might go back later for an afternoon session.

His pulse kicked up a notch as he approached the house next door. He hardly knew his neighbors and wasn't sure what they would think of his getup. The single mom who lived there had never even spoken to him, and her daughters were quiet as mice.

If the girls hadn't left a letter in Brian's mailbox last week, he wouldn't have considered buying them gifts. When he found the envelope, addressed to the North Pole, he'd opened it to investigate. At first he'd assumed that the girls had mistaken his mailbox for their own, because the two were side by side. Then he read the letter and realized that they hadn't wanted their mother to see it.

The girls had penned the note to Santa in simple words and neat sentences. Judging by her careful signature, Mandy was the older daughter. Her sister, Alyssa, had scrawled her name at the bottom of the page in pink crayon. They asked for a couple of moderately priced toys that "Mommy can't buy this year."

Brian could easily afford the extra gifts; he had very few family members to shop for. But the last item on the list was something that no one could deliver—not even Santa. He'd been touched by the request and felt a powerful compulsion to make his neighbors' holiday a little brighter.

They could all use some cheering up.

bright sunshine and absent marine layer, it was going to be another unseasonably warm day.

The girls were on winter break for another week, and she'd promised them a trip to the beach. In her old life, she'd have gone shopping on the day after Christmas. Her world had changed so much that she didn't miss spending money. And she certainly didn't miss the credit card bills or the arguments with John.

When they first met, his success had impressed her. She'd grown up in a financially unstable household, so it was comforting to date someone rich. He'd spoiled her with expensive gifts and told her to never worry about a thing.

A few years after they got married, his career took a nosedive and their relationship followed suit. He hid his gambling addiction from her and lied about his whereabouts. Soon the facade came tumbling down.

If he hadn't been murdered, she'd have filed for divorce. He'd refused to face their problems and never acknowledged that he needed help.

He wouldn't let her in.

John's death hadn't been easier to deal with because she'd fallen out of love with him. Failing marriage or not, Leah had depended on him. He'd abandoned them and left her to pick up the pieces, and she still resented him for it.

Leah made breakfast for the girls, who couldn't wait to walk down to the shore. They'd been in this house for several months, and although the beach was only two blocks away, they hadn't spent much time there.

"Can we wear our suits?" Mandy asked.

"I suppose," Leah said, smothering a surge of anxiety. Both girls had taken swimming lessons, but they were small, and the Pacific Ocean was dangerous. "We're just going to get our feet wet."

That was good enough for them. While they ran to their room to don their bathing suits, Leah packed a bag with snacks, drinks and towels. She didn't have any beach toys, so she grabbed her gardening tools and put them in a small plastic bucket.

When they were ready, she ushered the kids outside, locked the door and set the alarm behind her. Brian was in his driveway, scrubbing down his work truck with a long brush. He was wearing gray cargo shorts and a faded red T-shirt.

She couldn't ignore him like she used to, so she waved hello.

"What are you girls up to?" he asked with an easy smile, turning off the water faucet.

"We're going to the beach!" Alyssa said.

His eyes traveled along Leah's legs, which hadn't seen the light of day, or felt the heat of a man's gaze, in a long time. "My favorite place," he said, clearing his throat. He winked at Mandy. "Have fun."

She expected one of her daughters to invite him along. When they didn't, Leah urged them forward, feeling like she'd dodged a bullet. But every step she took away from him made her insides twist with guilt.

"Wait," she said, tugging on Alyssa's hand.

Mandy stopped her forward march. "What?"

She turned to look at Brian again. He was wiping down the interior of his truck, studiously ignoring her. "Would you like to come with us?"

His hands stilled and he glanced over his shoulder.

Leah wasn't surprised when Mandy and Alyssa started jumping up and down in agreement. They lived an isolated existence. The prospect of hanging out with anyone besides their mother was wildly exciting.

"Okay," he said, tossing aside a dust cloth. Just like that, he slammed the driver's side door of his truck and followed them to the beach.

They lived a few blocks from a long, narrow stretch of coastline known as The Strand. Several miles of road ran parallel to the beach, offering drivers a scenic view of girls in bikinis. Teenagers and rubberneckers drove up and down the strip every day of the week, checking out the hotties. Between the street and the beach there was a barrier of large, slate-colored rocks, mixed with heavy chunks of concrete. During high tide, the waves met these rocks and the beach all but disappeared.

Leah knew that because last time they'd had to walk all the way to the pier to find enough space to lay down a towel.

Today there was a nice amount of sand and it wasn't too crowded. Leah pointed to a spot near the lifeguard tower and they headed toward it.

"Is the tide coming in?" she asked Brian.

"Going out," he said.

There were some advantages to bringing a surfer along, she supposed. If one of her children got knocked down by a wave, he could save them.

Fortunately, the ocean looked peaceful at the moment. There were no powerful breakers churning up the sand. Soft waves lapped at the shore, barely causing a stir. "Did you go surfing this morning?"

He shook his head. "Nothing to ride."

She glanced out at the gentle water. "Oh, of course. Silly question."

"Not at all."

"Well, I obviously don't know anything about the ocean."

"You didn't grow up here."

"Right." And this was why she avoided people. Pretty soon he'd ask where she was from. "Did you?"

"Yes. Born and raised. Although raised is too kind a word to describe my upbringing. 'Turned loose' might be more accurate."

"Why's that?"

"I was a foster kid. My sister and I both were."

Leah came to a stop near the shore, spreading out her towel and spraying the girls down with sunscreen. "Can we build sand castles?" Mandy asked. When Leah said yes, they grabbed the bucket of tools and started digging.

Alyssa got upset when her first tower crumbled.

"You need to pack it down," Brian explained, helping her fill the cup again. He patted the sand with the flat of his hand, showing her. She turned it upside down and lifted the cup, delighted with the smooth-set formation.

While Alyssa and Leah made a grand sand castle, Mandy and Brian started digging a moat the size of a small pond. Soon it was a major building project, complete with a seaweed drawbridge and pebble walkway.

The girls were covered in sand by the time they were finished, so Leah took them to rinse off in the ocean. Although the water was very cold, they splashed in the shallow surf, chasing each other along the shore.

Brian smiled at their antics. "Do they ever get tired?"

"Not as often as I'd like," she admitted.

He wore a mild expression, sympathy mixed with envy.

"Why don't you have any children of your own?"

His brows rose at the question.

Leah flushed, realizing she was being nosy. "I'm sorry."

"No, it's fine. I just don't know how to answer that without making you uncomfortable."

"You don't have to," she said quickly, trying to squelch her curiosity. "It was rude of me to ask."

He laughed, shoving his hands into his pockets. "Your girls are lucky."

She watched her daughters play. They hadn't looked so carefree in a long time. "Why do you say that?"

"Because you never take your eyes off them."

"I wish I could," she murmured. "I fret too much."

At that exact moment, Alyssa tripped and fell face-first into the water. Leah bolted into motion, running to her daughter and hauling her upright. Alyssa sputtered and coughed, gasping for breath. When her airway cleared, she started bawling.

Leah hugged Alyssa to her chest, cradling her bedraggled head. Her little body was shivering, sobs wrenching from her throat. She carried Alyssa back to the towel and wrapped her up in it, murmuring soft words of comfort. Brian handed another towel to Mandy and they sat together until Alyssa's tears subsided.

He didn't seem bothered by the minor incident. John had often accused her of babying the girls, but Leah had never been able to ignore their cries. She took an orange out of her bag, peeling it for Alyssa. "Okay now?"

She nodded, accepting a fruit slice. Mandy also wanted some. They ate the sweet, tart sections while the sun warmed their skin.

Leah offered Brian another orange, which he declined.

"Do you want to walk down the jetty?" he asked.

Leah eyed the man-made rock pathway that jutted out into the ocean. She'd seen fishermen casting poles from its jagged sides, and waves sloshing over the rocks, threatening to drag unsuspecting beachgoers out to sea.

"Mom's afraid of water," Mandy announced.

Brian glanced at Leah in surprise.

She peeled the second orange, her cheeks heating. "I don't like deep water. Or big waves."

"How big?"

"Over my head."

"Those are the best kind."

"For surfing, you mean?"

"Yeah. The bigger the wave, the better the ride. They go fast and break clean. And deep water is much less dangerous to wipe out in."

She ate another slice of orange. "That makes sense."

"Can you swim?"

"No," she admitted. "The girls have taken lessons but I...can't bring myself to."

He gave her a curious look. "Is it just the ocean you're afraid of, or all water?"

"All water, I guess. Lakes, oceans...swimming pools." Before he could ask where her fear originated, she steered the conversation in a different direction. "Why do you like surfing so much?"

"I'll tell you on the way to the jetty," he said, jerking his chin toward it. "The waves aren't even knee-high today. It's perfectly safe."

She rose, brushing the sand off her bottom. "All right."

Mandy leapt to her feet. Alyssa forgot her tears and ran along the shore with her sister. It was about a quarter mile to the jetty so they had a few minutes to talk. The girls were within shouting distance, but couldn't overhear their quiet conversation.

Leah crossed her arms over her chest, aware that the front of her tank top was damp from hugging Alyssa. Although she had a bra on, the white fabric looked transparent and she felt self-conscious.

Brian averted his eyes, as if he'd noticed her wet shirt but was too polite to stare. "One of my mom's boyfriends taught me to surf," he said, hands in his pockets. "It was the first time I remember feeling safe."

She studied his face, unable to fathom an experience so opposite her own. Her *worst* childhood memory involved water.

"Out there, it's quiet. Peaceful. You're with other people, but alone. You have to be patient and wait for the right wave to come along. There's no rushing, no pushing. Another surfer can drop in on you and steal your turn, but that's rare, and it's impossible to paddle close enough to get in a fistfight."

Leah wondered if he'd grown up in an abusive home. She couldn't imagine feeling more at ease in a turbulent ocean than on land. Troubled past aside, he had a calming presence and exuded self-confidence. His easy manner, matched with that unflinching honesty, made him seem kind of invincible.

Some men grew stronger through adversity.

"I first started surfing to escape my problems. Now I think it helps me deal with them. I always feel better when I come in from a session."

"Cooking is like that for me."

"Is it?"

"Yes. I have certain dishes I make when I need to sort out my thoughts. I like to let my mind go blank and just focus on the task."

He nodded, pleased that she understood.

"What happened to your mom's boyfriend?" she asked.

"I don't know. He wasn't around for long, but he left a hell of a lot better impression than the others. I was sorry to see him go."

When they arrived at the jetty, Brian climbed onto the path ahead of Mandy while Leah trailed after them, holding Alyssa's hand. Being near deep water always made her uneasy, but his relaxed attitude reassured her.

He hadn't laughed at her or dismissed her fears. Without pushing, he'd encouraged her to step out of her comfort zone.

Maybe some of his assuredness would rub off on her.

They walked to the end of the jetty, watching power-boats and ocean barges in the distance. Leah picked up Alyssa, propping her on one hip. Brian put his hand on Mandy's shoulder, pointing toward the rippling water. "Look, a dolphin."

"Where?" she asked, searching the horizon.

"Just past that orange buoy."

While they waited, breathless, the dolphin arced across the surface again. A second dolphin followed close behind, its curved back glimmering in the sun.

"Another one," Mandy said.

Alyssa gasped. "I see it!"

Leah's eyes met Brian's and they smiled, sharing the moment of wonder. Her heart did a funny little jump inside her chest, half pain, half joy. She wished John was here beside her, but doubted he'd have appreciated the sight.

Swallowing hard, she tore her gaze away. It seemed strange to enjoy another man's company, and unfair to compare him to her husband. She'd been unhappy with John and she hardly knew Brian.

Nor could she get to know him. In the past twenty-four hours, they'd exchanged a meal and shared some very personal information. It was almost as if they'd skipped the acquaintance stage—and she wasn't supposed to make close connections.

She certainly couldn't risk being *more* than friends.

Her pulse throbbed with the realization that the idea appealed to her. He was handsome and compelling, an irresistible combination of light and dark. He had strong, callused hands. She wanted him to touch her.

"I have to go," she blurted.

If he was disappointed by her announcement, he didn't show it. They headed back and the girls danced along the shore once again, kicking up sand and saltwater. Leah avoided Brian's gaze and he made no attempt to engage her in conversation.

He didn't speak at all until they reached his front walk. "Thanks for bringing me along," he said. "It was nice."

Mandy and Alyssa ran next door and started ringing the bell for fun, a move that never failed to exasperate Leah.

Brian took one look at her annoyed expression and laughed. "They like to try your patience."

"Constantly."

"It's a good sign. Kids are supposed to misbehave."

Leah thought it might be a sign of lax discipline, but she kept that to herself. It was clear that he preferred her parenting style over whatever he'd experienced as a child. At best, he'd been neglected.

"Why don't you let me give you a swimming lesson?"

"Stop that!" she called out to the girls, dodging his question. The idea of diving into the ocean terrified her.

"I know a place with a heated pool. No big waves."

"That's a very kind offer, but I can't."

His eyes drifted south, settling on her damp tank top for a split second before rising back to her face. "Okay."

She forced a smile. Although she wanted to linger, she said goodbye and hurried away. Every moment she spent with him made her long for another, and she couldn't bear to pin her heart on false hopes.

She'd had enough loss in her life.

Chapter 4

The week passed quickly.

Leah kept busy with the girls, taking them to the park and the movies and even the San Diego Zoo. They enjoyed a glorious stretch of warm weather. The winter break would be over soon, so she was glad they'd made the most of their time.

Brian had been relegated to the back of her mind.

Mostly.

The girls spoke of him less often and no longer begged to pay him a visit. Like all children, they had short attention spans. Soon they would stop asking about him.

Leah couldn't forget him so easily. He'd always been visible, walking to the beach, working out of his truck. Now his presence seemed magnified. They exchanged polite smiles but avoided meaningful eye contact. It was difficult to pretend he wasn't there. She felt him, even when she couldn't see him. She wondered if he felt her.

By Friday afternoon she'd grown restless. Before Brian knocked on her door, her lackluster existence had been bearable. His vibrancy and strength made her long for the things she didn't know she'd missed.

Cooking usually improved her outlook, so she decided to go to the market. Maybe a plate of fun party snacks would fill the emptiness inside her. It was almost New Year's Eve. She could pretend she was hosting an upscale soiree.

Witnesses in the program were encouraged to change their regular routines. Other than dropping off the kids at school and showing up to work on time, Leah kept a random schedule. Her habits as Leanne Houck, like going to Starbucks every morning or wearing designer clothes, were not part of her new persona.

And she could no longer afford those luxuries she once took for granted. Shopping at Green Market was her one indulgence. She went there to buy fresh produce and quality ingredients every week or so.

This afternoon she had a hankering for fresh mozzarella and imported olives. The selection of goods varied by region, and the Oceanside store had more foreign items than her old standby in Kansas City. Leah grabbed a cart and strolled up and down the aisles, perusing the well-stocked shelves.

When Alyssa started fussing, Leah handed her a piece of sugar-free bubble gum from the bottom of her purse.

"No fair," Mandy said, stomping her foot. "I want one."

Leah couldn't find anything but a stray quarter. "You

can buy a gumball from the machine at the front of the store."

Alyssa tried to climb out of the cart. "Me, too!"

Sighing, Leah lifted her up and set her down. "Hold your sister's hand," she ordered Mandy. "And come right back."

They raced off.

"Walk!" she called after them, wincing at the loudness of her voice. She'd always admired serene parents but had no idea how to be one. It wasn't like she *wanted* to screech at her children in public.

Browsing the spices, she found a jar of saffron. There was a round mirror on the wall across from her, placed high enough that the store owner could keep an eye on the customers. When Leah glanced up, intending to make sure the girls hadn't wandered too far, she caught a glimpse of a stocky man standing in the next aisle over.

He turned and walked away, but not before she saw his face.

It was Mariano Felix, her husband's killer.

The spice jar fell from her hand, shattering on the floor. Felix continued around the corner and disappeared.

Leah's heart seized in her chest. She'd only seen him for a split second. Was her mind playing tricks on her? Felix had distinctive wavy black hair and thick eyebrows. This man's hair was shorter but his features were the same.

Abandoning her cart, she ran toward the front of the store, looking for Mandy and Alyssa. No longer concerned with appearing calm, she yelled their names. They weren't at the candy machines near the entrance.

She spun around, searching the immediate vicinity. People were staring at her.

When a man in a tie approached, blocking her view of the parking lot, she felt like shoving him out of the way. "Is there a problem, ma'am?"

"My daughters are missing!"

"I can page them on the loudspeaker," he said.

Leah didn't know what to do. She wasn't sure which direction they'd gone. What if Felix had followed them outside?

She was about to bolt through the front entrance, screaming bloody murder, when she saw two small, dark-haired heads by the restroom door. There was a drinking fountain against the far wall. Of course.

Mandy and Alyssa walked toward her, hand in hand.

"I see them," Leah said, nodding at the grocer. Instead of taking her children and leaving the store, she ducked into the bathroom with them, her pulse pounding. With shaking hands, she removed the cell phone from her purse and dialed the U.S. Marshals Service.

"What's wrong?" Mandy asked.

"Never do that again," Leah said, somewhere between furious and terrified. "I thought you'd been kidnapped!"

"Deputy Marshal Dominguez," a man answered.

"This is Leah Hansen," she said, lowering her voice and facing away from her daughters. "I just saw Felix."

"Where?"

"At Green Market on Mission Road. I'm still here, in the bathroom."

"What's his current location?"

"I don't know. He might be in the store."

"Okay," he said. "Sit tight. An officer will be there in a few minutes."

It was twenty minutes before Dominguez arrived, and by then Felix was long gone. Working in conjunction with the USMS, Oceanside Police evacuated the market and searched the premises, to no avail.

While a female officer watched over the girls, Leah was questioned in detail about the sighting. She repeated the same information over and over, growing less certain each time she gave the description.

"Are you sure it was him?" Dominguez asked.

"No," she said, rubbing her arms. It was cold in the store, and she couldn't stop shivering.

"Let me show you the video."

Leah watched footage from two separate cameras. Both were poor quality and neither had captured a good angle. The height and body type fit Mariano Felix, but there was no way to make a positive identification.

"I looked right at him in the mirror," she said again.

"The mirror distorts reflections."

He'd mentioned that already.

"I'll take the footage to tech support and try to have it cleaned up," Dominguez offered. "We'll also run the license plate numbers for all of the cars in the parking lot. Maybe we'll get lucky."

"Do I have to move again?" she asked.

His brows rose at the question. In the past eighteen months, they'd relocated her from Kansas City to Seattle, and from Seattle to Oceanside. "I doubt it. Sightings like this aren't uncommon, Leah. I'd like for you to speak with a psychologist—"

"You don't believe me?"

He gave her a reassuring smile. "We will investigate to the fullest. In the meantime, it's wise to exercise caution. A squad car will patrol your neighborhood over the weekend. You can meet with Dr. Phelps on Monday."

"Fine," she said, sighing. She didn't want to be relocated. She just wanted this nightmare to be over.

Brian washed and dried the plastic containers and put them back inside the red-striped gift bag Leah had given him.

He'd planned to leave the items on her doorstep. It was almost 9:00 p.m., pretty late for a family with young children, and it hadn't escaped his attention that she wasn't interested in continuing their acquaintance. But before he could set down the bag and walk away, she wrenched the door open.

Her gaze was wide-eyed and mildly accusatory. He wasn't surprised by that, having encountered her fierce protectiveness before. What knocked him for a loop, once again, was her beauty. Maybe because she appeared plain from a distance, he was fascinated by how striking she was up close.

Over the past week, he'd told himself that his memory had embellished the loveliness of her face or the shape of her breasts.

A quick glance down confirmed his recollection. The soft, loose shirt didn't quite camouflage her figure. He suspected she wasn't wearing a bra and might have been tempted to stare if he hadn't noticed a far more important detail: she looked distraught.

"What do you want?" she asked.

"Just to return this," he said, handing her the gift bag.

Accepting it, she peeked inside. "You didn't have to. The containers are disposable."

"Oh." Now he felt like an ass for disturbing her. "Well, thanks again for the invite. Everything was delicious."

Her eyes filled with tears.

Brian worried that she was going to break down in sobs the moment he walked away. "What's wrong?"

Shaking her head, she avoided his gaze.

"Is someone bothering you? Besides me, I mean."

She laughed at his self-deprecating humor. It was a strange, sad laugh, and an awkward moment, but some of the tension between them eased. "You're not bothering me," she said. "I just had a rough day."

"Tell me about it."

After a moment's deliberation, she waved him inside. "The girls are in bed already."

Brian's pulse jumped at the news. Her girls were great, but he liked the idea of being alone with her.

"If I had anything besides juice, I'd offer you a drink."

"I'm not much of a drinker," he said, shrugging. He bought a six-pack every so often, but never drank more than one at a time.

She sat down on the couch, gesturing for him to do the same. "I had a scare earlier."

His muscles tightened. "What kind of a scare?"

"Mandy and Alyssa walked away from me at the grocery store. When I went to look for them, I couldn't find them. I panicked."

"Where were they?"

"At the drinking fountain," she said, crossing her arms over her chest. "I felt this overpowering terror. I didn't know what to do, or where to start searching for them. And I didn't handle it well."

Brian's shoulders relaxed slightly. No one had hurt her or her children. "How did you handle it?"

"I ran around the store, screaming like a crazy woman."

He smiled at the obvious exaggeration.

"It's not funny," she said.

"No," he agreed, schooling his expression.

"I made a scene."

He studied her with interest, wondering why she disliked drawing attention to herself. She dressed to blend in and seemed uncomfortable with scrutiny. "Most mothers would react the same way."

She nibbled on her lower lip, appearing uncertain.

"My mom wouldn't, of course. But she made plenty of scenes. She collapsed in the grocery store once, if I remember correctly."

The blood drained from her cheeks. "Why?"

"Drugs, I suppose. I was only seven or eight, so the details are fuzzy. I remember watching her ride away in an ambulance."

"What did you do?"

"I stole a candy bar while everyone was distracted and walked home."

Her mouth dropped open.

"You take good care of your girls, Leah. My mother wouldn't even have noticed if my sister or I disappeared."

"I'm sorry," she said.

"Don't be. I turned out fine."

"Is your mother still alive?"

He nodded, glancing away. The irony of the situation wasn't lost on him. Brenda had been a loving, conscientious parent, like Leah. And yet, she'd died young while their drug-addled mom soldiered on. "It doesn't seem fair, does it?"

"No."

"Was your husband—" He cut himself off, realizing the inappropriateness of the question.

"Was he what?"

He bit the bullet. "Was he a good dad?"

"No," she admitted, after a short hesitation.

Brian stared at her in amazement. The answer was unexpected, but plainly sincere. "Why not?"

"He was a good man, and he loved the girls, but he gambled. The habit…devoured him. It took him away from us."

Her confession was like a punch in the gut. He didn't understand how a man could fail such a beautiful family.

"Sometimes I'm glad he's dead," she said, her voice flat. "Mandy and Alyssa weren't old enough to understand what he was going through. In their eyes, he was perfect. If he'd lived, I'm afraid he would have continually disappointed them."

He knew what she meant. In his twenties, he'd given up hope that his mother would change, but he'd never been able to stop caring about her. Even now, she had the power to let him down.

"You think I'm terrible."

"I'd be a hypocrite if I thought that."

She examined his face. "Is that why you were alone on Christmas? Being with your mother is too difficult?"

He leaned back against the couch, resting his arm on the frame. "It's difficult, yes. I haven't been in touch with her since Brenda's funeral. It was frustrating to see her grieve. Too little, too late, if that makes sense."

Her eyes softened with understanding.

"I also wanted to be alone this year. Or, I thought that was what I wanted."

"Why?"

"Christmas is always weird for me," he said. "I have a friend from the foster care system that I sometimes hang out with, but he got married last summer. This year he went with his wife to visit her family for the holidays."

"You've never been married?"

"No."

"What about a steady girlfriend?"

"No one lately," he said, feeling heat creep up his neck. He hoped she wouldn't ask how long he'd been sleeping alone. "My friend's wife has threatened to put my picture on an internet dating site."

She laughed, raking a hand through her hair. "You should let her."

Brian watched her intently, fascinated by every line of her face. He had no intention of allowing Gretchen to take over his love life. If he couldn't find a woman on his own, he didn't deserve one. "You should let me give you a swimming lesson."

She stopped laughing.

"It's easy."

"For you, maybe."

"If you were more comfortable in the water, you could relax at the beach." When she chewed on the edge of her thumbnail, wavering, he said, "You also need to know how to swim for your daughters' safety."

"Now you're giving me a guilt-trip."

"Whatever works."

"Where is this pool?"

"About ten minutes away. We'd have it all to ourselves. The girls can swim, too."

"They'd like that," she admitted.

He wished she'd say yes because she wanted to. "I can't imagine where I'd be if I never had that first surfing lesson. It changed my life."

She held up a hand to ward him off. "I'm never going surfing."

Laughing, he said, "But you'll try swimming?"

After a short pause, she nodded. "Okay."

He grinned, delighted to have talked her into it. "You'll be fine."

"I might freak out."

"Don't worry about it. We can take as many breaks as you need."

They made arrangements to leave before noon the next day, and she promised to pack a picnic lunch. Brian knew it wasn't a date, but he couldn't squelch the feeling of excitement and anticipation in his belly.

If he wasn't concerned about scaring her off again, he might have tried to kiss her good-night.

Leah locked the door behind Brian and set the alarm, her heart sinking.

Why had she agreed to go swimming?

After the afternoon she'd had, the last thing she wanted to do was stress out or make a fool of herself. She knew she couldn't tolerate being submerged in water. Tomorrow she was going to thrash and sputter like a wet cat.

She also felt conflicted about encouraging him. He looked at her in an appreciative, manly way and she liked it. She might have avoided eye contact with him this week but she hadn't been able to suppress her fantasies.

Late at night, in her bed, she thought about him.

Although he was very attractive, it wasn't just his looks that drew her in. His personality was irresistible. He seemed so...resilient. He'd had a hard life but he wasn't broken. In his presence, she felt safe.

Brian could help her overcome her fears.

If she learned to swim, she'd be taking a step forward, managing her anxiety. She felt like she had no control over her current situation. The program told her where to live, where to work. The lack of freedom, along with her frequent nightmares and constant worry about Mariano Felix, was crippling her.

Had she really seen him earlier? Or had he been a figment of her imagination, an apparition from a nightmare?

After checking in on the girls, who were sleeping soundly, she turned off the lights and crawled into bed. If she was being honest with herself, she'd admit that hooking up with Brian had some advantages. He wasn't the kind of man she would normally date, with his troubled past and iffy finances. But he was tall and intimidating-looking. He had hard muscles and strong hands.

Although all evidence showed that he was gentle with women and children, and sensitive to other people's feelings, she'd bet he could raise those hands to defend himself if push came to shove.

He could defend her, too.

She'd never considered getting a boyfriend for security purposes. Since John's death, she hadn't felt a flicker of interest in a man. Her children came first. Besides, it wasn't fair to get involved with someone under these circumstances. She was living under a false name, and could be relocated at the drop of a hat.

Now that she'd seen Felix—maybe—her outlook had shifted. She could use the extra protection. She needed to be proactive.

Hugging a pillow to her chest, she closed her eyes, imagining Brian in her bed.

Chapter 5

Leah spent half the night tossing and turning, torn between terrifying memories of Mariano Felix and sexy fantasies starring Brian Cosgrove.

Maybe she should cancel their swimming plans.

She couldn't believe she'd told him the truth about John. When he'd asked if her husband had been a good father, she should have said yes. Portraying John as an ideal partner would have discouraged Brian from entertaining romantic thoughts.

But she'd looked into his dark, earnest eyes and was unable to tell the lie. Now she felt overexposed, almost desperate. She might as well have complained about John's performance in their bedroom, which had become increasingly perfunctory.

They'd never been a perfect couple, just a pretty facade. And his secrets had weighed her down for so long. In the months before his murder, she'd wanted to tell her mother and her best friend about his gambling habit. Pride and shame held her back. Maybe if she'd been more honest, she could have built a support system. John's friends and family might have been able to convince him to seek help. Too late, she'd learned an important lesson about addiction: secrets keep people sick.

She spent most of the morning doing chores. It was New Year's Eve, and the kids would be going back to school on Monday. She'd return to work, decorating an endless assembly line of frozen cakes.

When the laundry was done and the dishes were put away, she told the girls that they were going to the pool with Brian. They cheered and danced around the living room before running to don their swimsuits. Leah made cucumber sandwiches and packed a Thermos of lemonade for their picnic lunch.

Stomach fluttering with anticipation, she searched her closet for her own bathing suit. Although she didn't swim, she owned a sleek navy one-piece for appearances' sake. John had often taken her to pool parties at the homes of his wealthy friends. She'd met Mariano Felix at one such occasion.

The navy suit wasn't as revealing as a bikini but it didn't exactly offer full coverage. Spaghetti straps crossed over her back and brief triangles of fabric cupped her breasts. It disguised some of her flaws, like the faint stretch marks on her lower abdomen, but also clung to every dip and curve of her body.

She didn't have anything else to swim in, and the style was modest by California standards, so she turned away from the mirror, slipping into a loose tunic and pulling on a pair of cutoff shorts.

When Brian appeared on the front step, they were

ready. Leah hitched her beach bag on one shoulder and went to the door.

"Hi, girls," he said, smiling at Mandy and Alyssa before he greeted Leah. His eyes crinkled at the corners and his teeth flashed white against his sun-dark skin. Something flowered inside her when his gaze met hers. Although they'd only known each other a short time, she felt connected to him in a way that went deeper than physical attraction. He was special, and tempting, and a little dangerous.

He'd talked her into a swimming lesson with almost no effort. She would have to work very hard to remain aloof.

"You didn't change your mind?"

"Not yet," she said, her cheeks growing warm. Taking Alyssa's hand, she shuffled out the door, locking it behind her.

"Do you mind if I ride with you?"

She shook her head, figuring that was best. Her car had the child safety seats and his work truck wouldn't fit them all. After she secured Alyssa and opened the door for Mandy, she climbed behind the wheel. Brian got in the passenger side, folding his long legs into the cramped space.

"You can move the seat back," Leah said.

He reclined a bit, careful not to crush Alyssa, whose car seat was directly behind him. Even after the adjustment, his knees touched the glove compartment, but he didn't complain. As she started the engine, Leah noted that he had muscular calves, lightly covered with dark hair. He wore his shorts long, almost over the knee. When he cleared his throat, she realized she'd been caught staring.

She turned her attention to the road. "Where are we going?"

He gave her directions to a house near Tourmaline Beach. It was a short drive down the freeway, followed by a twisty path along the coastal cliffs. The girls chattered nonstop and asked Brian about a thousand silly questions.

"It's this driveway, on your left," he said, pointing to a nice house tucked into the hillside. There was a small, shady front yard and a two-car garage. Leah parked in the driveway and they all got out.

"Who lives here?"

"No one, right now," he said, taking a set of keys out of his pocket. "The couple that rented it for the holidays left early."

Leah assumed that one of his customers owned the house, which was modern and spacious inside. There were stylish, comfortable furnishings but no framed photographs or cozy personal touches. "Did you do work here?" she asked, smoothing her palm over a sleek granite countertop.

"Yes, actually. I put in a new bathroom and remodeled the kitchen."

Leah was impressed. The kitchen was fit for a chef, with dark cherry cabinets and stainless steel appliances. "Nice."

"Thanks."

"Is that what you're doing in the house next door?" It hadn't occurred to her before now that Brian wasn't a permanent resident in her neighborhood.

He took the packed lunches from Leah and stashed them in the fridge. "I'm working on a top-to-bottom overhaul for that place. And the buyer demographic is different, so I have to use less expensive materials to keep the cost down."

She was surprised by how knowledgeable he sounded. Maybe that talk of digging trenches had thrown her off. "Price was no object for this owner?"

His lips curved into a smile. "I didn't say that. He got a good deal on the labor."

Mandy and Alyssa pressed their faces against the sliding glass door, admiring the sparkling blue pool in the backyard. Brian led them outside, where both girls kicked off their flip-flops, giggling with excitement.

Leah wasn't looking forward to taking off her outerwear and slipping into the water. To her relief, she didn't have to. While she fit Alyssa with a safety jacket, Brian tossed aside his shirt and dove in. Mandy swam well enough that she didn't need a vest. She plugged her nose and hopped into the pool with a splash.

When Brian resurfaced, pushing his dark hair off his forehead, he gestured for Alyssa to come to him. Leah swung her out, into his arms. Alyssa screamed in delight as he caught her, showing none of her mother's trepidation.

Brian entertained the girls for over an hour. They jumped off the diving board, swam like little fish and played water games. Leah watched from the sidelines, wishing she could have half as much fun in the water. By the time they broke for lunch, Mandy and Alyssa were pink-cheeked from exertion, and Leah hadn't even gotten her feet wet.

She wasn't able to relax, exactly, but it was no hardship to study Brian's rippling muscles and bronzed skin. He was also a natural with kids. His relaxed attitude and obvious lust for life made him an irresistible playmate. Some men acted clownish and overenthusiastic with children. Others, like John, were too distracted or self-absorbed. Brian's laid-back personality was a good fit for Mandy and Alyssa.

Leah hadn't been the liveliest, most energetic mom lately. It was clear by the way the girls interacted with Brian that they were starved for attention.

They both had voracious appetites at lunch, as well. After they were finished, Alyssa looked sleepy. Deciding that the girls needed a break, Leah sat them down on the couch in front of the television.

"I think there's a kid movie in here," Brian said, searching the DVD cabinet. *"Princess and the Frog?"*

"They love that one," Leah said.

He put it on for them, giving Leah a weighted glance. She wasn't going to be let off the hook for the swimming lesson.

"Keep an eye on your sister," Leah told Mandy, even though she'd be able to see them from the pool. Dropping a kiss on Alyssa's damp head, she walked back outside, following Brian across the patio.

He did a backflip off the edge of the pool, landing with an inelegant splash.

"Showoff," Leah muttered, removing her blouse and shorts. She didn't know what she was more nervous about, getting in the water with him or baring her skin.

He hadn't ogled her in front of the kids, but he wasn't above checking her out now that they had a modicum of privacy. His gaze traveled along the curves of her body, darkening with appreciation.

Leah flushed and clenched her fists at her sides, stifling the urge to cover her breasts with her hands. Although she didn't have much to hide, and the swimsuit flattered her slim figure, she felt intensely self-conscious.

"Okay, pretty lady," he said, flashing a wolfish grin. "Get over here."

She descended the stairs into the pool, trying to stay calm. He wasn't taking this too seriously and that helped settle her nerves. The water was heated to a comfortable temperature, but still felt cool and refreshing.

When her toes touched the bottom, she stood waist-deep in the shallow end. He hovered near the middle of the pool, waiting for her. Watching her face. Her pulse jettisoned as she moved toward him, her bare feet skimming the tiled surface. Soon the water level rose above her shoulders, almost to her chin.

She stopped and gripped the coping, short of breath.

He seemed to realize that she'd reached her limit. "Can you tread water?" he asked, demonstrating the technique.

"No."

"Float on your back?"

Her stomach dropped at the thought. She shook her head, shivering.

"Blow bubbles?" Dipping his nose and mouth under the surface, he showed her what he meant.

The girls had mastered bubbles as toddlers, so Leah was familiar with this basic first step to swimming. For her, it was an insurmountable obstacle. Memories came flooding back to her, along with the sickening smell of chlorine. She pictured her body thrashing as she tried to claw her way to the surface.

"I can't," she said.

He straightened, sluicing water from his face. "It's okay. You're doing great."

"I haven't done anything yet."

"You got in."

She inclined her head in acknowledgment. This was

an uncommon feat for her. If not for his distracting hotness, she might not have come this far. Tearing her gaze away, she glanced back at the house, checking on the girls.

"They're fine," he said.

"Is the front door locked?"

"Yes."

She turned her attention back to Brian, who radiated strength and confidence. "I haven't been in a pool since I was a kid."

"Why don't you tell me what happened?"

Her fingernails dug into the coping. "It's not that big a deal."

"You might feel better if you talk about it. Learning to swim isn't just a physical thing. Your head has to be in it."

Leah thought about other physical activities that didn't work unless the participants were mentally into it. The corner of Brian's mouth tipped up, as if his mind had traveled a similar direction.

"Think of it as a trust-building exercise," he said. "We're not going to get very far unless you open up a little. Your stories can't be any worse than mine."

She nibbled on her lower lip, deliberating. That was true. Nothing in her childhood compared to the few details he'd told her about his. And yet, he seemed content and well-adjusted, while she was a nervous wreck.

In her defense, she'd witnessed a murder.

Secrets keep people sick, she reminded herself. There was no reason to hide this one any longer. "My parents traveled around a lot when I was a kid," she said. "They flitted from one city to another, and must been involved with a dozen get-rich quick schemes. I lived with my cousins, off and on."

"Boy cousins?" he asked, his eyes narrowing.

"Two boys and a girl. They were wealthy but we had almost no supervision. My aunt was very...distant."

He fell silent, waiting for her to continue.

"The first summer I stayed with them I was about seven. They had a huge swimming pool. One day everyone was splashing around in the water, acting crazy. Someone pushed me into the deep end." She swallowed hard, her insides churning. "I went under and couldn't seem to find my way back up. There were thrashing legs and arms everywhere. I remember getting kicked in the throat."

"How did you get out?"

"I don't know. I woke up by the side of the pool, vomiting water. My cousins said if I told anyone what happened, they'd drown me on purpose."

"And you never tried to swim again," Brian concluded.

"Right."

"Where are these cousins now? In jail?"

She laughed, shaking her head. "I have no idea. We didn't stay in touch."

"Did they terrorize you in other ways?"

"No. They ignored me. Looking back on it, I think the experience was more traumatic because I felt abandoned by my parents. Their irresponsible decisions and selfishness caused the real damage. My cousins were just kids." It occurred to her that John's gambling addiction and subsequent death had triggered the same feelings. She'd married a man just like her parents without knowing it. That was pretty sad.

And now she was in another situation she had no control over, barely keeping her head above water. Mariano Felix wanted her dead. The Program ruled her life, and

Leah couldn't stand being helpless. Learning to swim seemed like a way to win her power back. Spending time with Brian also made her feel stronger.

She couldn't speak to any of her family members or close friends. She missed companionship and personal connections.

"You're doing better already," Brian said.

Leah realized she'd let go of the coping. Her first instinct was to grab it again, but she didn't give in, focusing on Brian instead.

"We really have to tackle breathing first. If you're not comfortable underwater you'll never be a strong swimmer."

She glanced back at the house, noting that both girls were absorbed in the movie. Although she was trying to lead by example, and face her challenges head-on, she didn't want them to see her flailing.

"Let's start with your mouth," he said. "Just put your lips in the water and blow. You don't even have to get your nose wet."

Leah studied his demonstration, noting that he had a well-shaped mouth. Not too full or soft-looking. She let her lips sink below the surface and blew bubbles. When the water tickled her nose, she startled, reaching for the coping again.

He covered her hand with his, peeling it from the railing. "Stay with me," he said, making eye contact. "You're doing fine."

She tried to concentrate on Brian. Unfortunately, she was assaulted by the memory of kicking legs and floating rafts.

He framed her face with his other hand and touched his wet lips to hers, shocking her out of the flashback. His mouth was calm and firm and deliciously grounding. For a split second, heat sparked between them. Then he pulled away.

"Now your nose," he said, as if he hadn't just kissed her. "Put it in the water and exhale. As long as you don't breathe in, no water will enter your airway."

"I can't," she said.

"You can."

She lifted her fingertips to her lips, which tingled with sensation. His kiss had distracted her so much that she was able to set aside her fear. Lowering her face into the water, she exhaled rapidly and rose up, victorious.

"Good," he said, smiling. "Do it again."

The next time was easier. She didn't sputter or choke.

"Now hold your breath and go under completely. Get your hair wet."

Taking a deep breath, she squeezed her eyes shut and went down. Water swirled in her ears and her hair floated around her head. The feeling was intensely foreign, after years of not swimming.

Gasping and floundering, she broke the surface. "I need to get out."

"Wait," he said, sliding his hand around the nape of her neck. Once again, he lowered his mouth to hers, kissing her gently. She struggled, still in the grips of panic. Then his tongue heated the seam of her lips and she parted them hesitantly, letting him in. Her first thought was that he didn't taste like John. His mouth was firmer, his motions less practiced. The scrape of his jaw felt rougher.

She relaxed and slipped her arms around his shoulders, digging her fingernails into his wet skin.

He ended the kiss.

Leah blinked up at him, her heart racing. She didn't

want to swim anymore. She wanted to thread her fingers through his hair and pull his mouth back down to hers.

She turned toward the house with a guilty flush, worried that the girls had seen the kiss. But neither was paying them any attention. When she returned her gaze to Brian, his eyes were locked on her lips. She moistened them, tasting him.

"This time we'll go under together," he said. "Hold your breath."

He didn't give her a chance to refuse. She inhaled on reflex and clung to his neck as they submerged. It was easier with him. Safer, somehow. After they came back up, he repeated the action, over and over, until she felt comfortable.

"This is working," she said, delighted.

Seeming pleased by her progress, he released her. "Try it on your own. Swimming is usually a solitary sport."

She wasn't as confident without him, but she managed to sink below the surface and come back up by herself a number of times. With the biggest obstacle behind her, the rest of the lesson went quickly. She learned to tread water, glide and kick her legs. As long as they didn't move to the deep end, she could stay calm. It helped to know that she could reach the side of the pool and touch the bottom.

Brian was another secure, solid object she could depend on.

"Let's work on floating," he said, placing his hand on the small of her back. At his urging, she reclined in the water. The position felt strange, like sleeping on the surface. "Fill your lungs with air and stick your chest out."

Leah trembled with self-consciousness. The fabric

of her swimsuit was thin, clinging to her breasts. How could she stick her chest out?

He splayed his hand over her spine, encouraging her to arch her back. "Look up at the sky and try to relax."

She took another breath and stared at the clouds, embarrassed. The air was cool against the front of her swimming suit, causing her nipples to pebble. Heat radiated from his fingertips and water lapped at her sides.

"Perfect," he said, moving his hand away.

Leah was able to hold the pose for a few seconds at the most. When his gaze dragged down her chest, she lost focus. Feeling overexposed, she rounded her shoulders and sank like a stone.

Her hands and feet found no purchase as she slipped down deeper. She screamed, releasing a flurry of bubbles.

Brian grabbed her by the arm and hauled her upright. She coughed and wheezed, her mind blank with fright. "I've got you," he said, holding her close. "Sorry about that. I guess I let go too soon."

He stroked her hair until her fear abated. Looking up at him, she slid her hand along his sculpted triceps, shivering.

With a groan, he set her aside, putting some space between them. "I think I'd get too distracted to finish the lesson if I kissed you again."

The raw desire in his voice gave her a feminine thrill. She liked knowing that he was tempted by her.

"Let's try one more time. I'll keep my hand underneath you."

She lay back again, aware that his eyes were on her body. Focusing on the heat smoldering between them, instead of her anxiety, she looked up at the sky and kept her spine straight, holding the position as long as she could. His hand fell away from her but she knew he was there if she needed him.

"Good," he said, a smile stretching across his face. "I knew you could do it."

They practiced floating until she got the hang of it. When the lesson was over, she felt proud of herself. She hadn't mastered any of the skills, but she hadn't given up, either. Her anxiety wasn't preventing her from learning.

Someday she might be able to swim in the ocean.

"Thank you," she said to Brian, giving him an impulsive hug. "You're a great teacher."

He shrugged off the compliment. "It's nothing. I just love the water."

She lifted her hand to his cheek, enjoying the grain of his beard stubble against her palm. His eyelids grew heavy as she brushed her lips over his, very tenderly. "My kids aren't watching us, are they?"

He looked at the house. "No."

Threading her fingers through his wet hair, she deepened the kiss, flicking her tongue against his. Groaning, he pinned her against the side of the pool and plundered her mouth, his hands skimming down her body. She pressed her breasts to his chest and wrapped her legs around his waist, squirming for more. He cupped her bottom with his big hands, fitting his erection against the cleft of her sex.

She gasped into his mouth, going still.

He broke the kiss, panting. "Too much?"

If Mandy and Alyssa weren't close by, she might have let him continue. Her body was aching for his touch, her nipples tightly beaded.

"Sorry," he said, releasing her. "I got a little carried away."

She pushed herself out of the pool, sitting on the edge. He studied the clingy fabric of her swimsuit as water streamed down her skin. Her chest rose and fell with every breath. "Don't be sorry," she said. "I liked it."

He tore his gaze away from her. "Damned heated pool."

Laughing, she raked a hand through her hair. "I should check on the girls."

"I'll stay here."

She smiled apologetically, realizing he needed a moment to recover. It was flattering to be lusted after by a man like him. "You're cute."

He groaned, sinking under the surface.

Still laughing, she rose to her feet and walked into the house, feeling happier than she had in a long time.

Chapter 6

Brian settled in a lounge chair, watching Leah and the girls splash in the water.

Mandy and Alyssa had wanted to swim again after the movie. They'd both squealed with excitement when Leah said she'd join them in the pool. As the sun crept lower in the sky, Mandy did a creative water ballet while Alyssa jumped off the edge, over and over again, into her mother's arms.

He couldn't stop staring at her.

The first time he'd seen Leah up close, she'd been frantic and accusatory, and he'd still thought her beautiful. Right now, she was breathtaking. Her blue eyes sparkled with affection as she smiled at her daughters. She hugged Alyssa to her chest and spun her around in the water, making her squeal out loud.

When she caught his gaze, she mouthed *thank you*.

Brian's chest tightened with emotion and he glanced

away, trying to hold himself together. It seemed impossible that a woman like her would want to hang out with him. She'd shared a painful piece of her past and trusted him with her safety in the water. Not only that, she'd let him kiss her. She'd kissed him back.

Leah was a great mom and a lovely, sensual woman. He couldn't believe she was here in his swimming pool, thanking *him*.

The pleasure was all his.

He tried not to think about the sweetness of her mouth or the feel of her body against his. The sun was still warm, making his muscles languid. Getting his desire under control after the swimming lesson had required a superhuman effort.

"Let's dry off," Leah said, helping Alyssa up the stairs. "We don't want to outwear our welcome."

Brian wouldn't have minded if they moved in. Not only was Leah irresistible, but her girls were special in their own right. Alyssa was a cute little imp and Mandy had a quiet grace that reminded him of Leah. Both were dark-eyed, presumably like their father, and had hair that was a richer brown than Leah's.

It disturbed him to know that her husband had been dragged down by gambling. He'd always been bothered by men who took their families for granted. Maybe because he'd never had one of his own. He'd have cherished the gift.

Leah rubbed the girls dry with towels and wrapped them both up, sitting them down on the opposite lounge chair. She grabbed her Thermos of lemonade and poured them each a plastic cup. When caring for her daughters, she was poised and sometimes stern, but never harsh. Brian studied her slender form while her back was turned, noting that she was curvier than her loose clothes suggested. She had shapely hips and a pert bottom. The wet fabric of her swimsuit left little to the imagination.

He tore his gaze away, contemplating another dip in the pool. Unfortunately, the water wasn't any colder than the air.

After they were dry, Leah took the girls inside for a bathroom break. Brian put his shirt on and followed her, wishing they could stay for dinner. Although they'd already spent most of the day together, he was reluctant to part ways.

He'd been using the house as a vacation rental, so the fridge was empty. When Leah reappeared with her daughters, fully clothed, he got a better idea. "Why don't we stop at a restaurant on the way home? My treat."

Her brows, which were a shade lighter than her hair, drew together. "You don't have to take us out."

"I want to. Besides, you provided lunch."

She waved a hand in the air. "Just sandwiches."

They were gourmet-delicious, like everything else she made. "There's a steak house down the street."

"Sounds expensive."

"Not really. It's a family place, very casual." He glanced down at his old T-shirt and board shorts, realizing he should change. "I have some jeans upstairs. And we can take my SUV, if you'd like. It's parked in the garage."

She gave him an incredulous look. "This is your house?"

He glanced around, nodding.

"What about the place next door to me?"

"I own that, too."

"You said you dig ditches."

"Yeah, well. They don't dig themselves."

She rummaged through her beach bag, finding her keys. "We'll have dinner at home. Are you ready to go?"

Brian could have driven himself, but it would be a hassle to keep two vehicles at the fixer-upper. He opened the door for Leah and the girls, locking it behind him.

It was clear that Leah was upset about something. He had no idea what, and he wasn't going to press her for details in front of the kids. Alyssa hopped and skipped down the sidewalk, unaware of the tension, but Mandy's mouth was downturned as she climbed into her car seat. She knew her mother's mood had changed.

For the next ten minutes, Brian wondered where he'd gone wrong. Maybe Leah was sick of his company. It had been a long day. Maybe she felt guilty for making out with him in the swimming pool. She was a fairly recent widow. Her husband didn't deserve her loyalty, from what Brian could tell, but even if he'd been a great guy, Leah was a young, beautiful woman. Who would expect her to grieve forever?

Disturbed by the sudden chill between them, he stared out the window in silence. They were falling into an unhealthy pattern. Whenever he got too close, she retreated. That wasn't working for him.

He hoped he'd get the chance to talk to her in private. If she refused to see him again, he'd be crushed. In a short time, he'd become completely infatuated with her. The emotional connection had snuck up him.

Why hadn't he been more guarded?

He knew better than to lose his head over woman who wasn't interested in getting involved. She'd been distant all week. Then, last night and today, she'd opened up again, sharing intimate personal details. Those moments had encouraged him.

The way she'd responded to his kiss had also encouraged him. He hadn't imagined her moaning and digging her nails into his back.

Damn it.

When they arrived on Surfrider Way, he helped Alyssa out of her car seat and carried Leah's beach bag to the front step. She ushered the girls inside and paused in the doorway to disengage a security alarm. "Go wash up for dinner."

"Is Brian going to eat with us?" Mandy asked.

"We'll see," Leah said, obviously meaning no. They raced down the hallway and she stepped back outside with him, closing the door behind her.

He waited for her to speak.

"You lied to me," she said.

"What?"

"You pretended you were poor." She gestured at his beat-up truck and faded T-shirt, as if they were evidence of his deception. "Your hands feel like sandpaper!"

Brian flushed at the criticism. He wasn't ashamed of his calluses, his work truck or his worn clothes. They were part of who he was. Success hadn't erased his past or softened his rough edges. "I haven't told you any lies."

She crossed her arms over her chest. "I asked if you'd done work at that house, and you spoke as if the owner wasn't you."

"That was a joke," he said, raking his hand through his hair. "I didn't mean to give you the wrong impression, and I wasn't trying to hide anything. I thought it was kind of cute that you didn't realize the house was mine."

"Cute?" Her expression was skeptical.

"Yeah. I liked that you were interested in me, not my finances."

"I felt sorry for you!"

Ouch. He looked away, shaking his head. "Sympathy is the last thing I want from a woman."

"You deliberately misled me."

"The hell I did," he said, lowering his voice. "You made assumptions based on my appearance and the type of work I do. Maybe you're used to men who brag about money and drive flashy cars. That's not me. I *like* getting my hands dirty. At the end of the day, they wash as clean as anyone else's."

She opened her mouth to reply, and then closed it.

"You seem bothered by the fact that I make a comfortable living. Did you feel safer, thinking you were above me?"

When her eyes filled with tears, he knew he'd crossed the line. He also thought he'd hit the nail on the head. But it wasn't like him to argue with a woman, and he cared about this one. Although she'd insulted him and called him a liar, he still wanted her. Those harsh words didn't seem as important as the kisses they'd shared or the meaningful glances they'd exchanged.

What did he care if she'd preferred him as a bum?

"I'm sorry," he said, lifting his hand to her face.

She turned her head to the side, shying away from his touch. "I'm sorry, too." Murmuring goodbye, she went into the house and shut the door behind her.

Leah felt awful about what she'd said to Brian.

She knew she'd overreacted to the news that he wasn't destitute. Her scathing comments had obviously hurt his pride. The worst part was that he'd been right.

She was mad at him for keeping secrets, but what bothered her most was the newly leveled playing field.

She *had* felt superior to him. When she'd thought Brian was poor, using him for protection seemed like fair game. She wasn't opposed to having a casual fling with a down-on-his-luck surfer. He wasn't appropriate for a serious relationship, so there was no danger of getting attached.

Now that she knew Brian was long-term material, she had to be more careful about getting emotionally involved. To her dismay, she already felt attached. She didn't know what she'd do if the Witness Protection Program relocated her again. If Mariano Felix was really on her trail, she could kiss Brian goodbye.

It was better to keep her distance and protect her heart.

Mandy and Alyssa went to bed early, exhausted from the long day in the sun. Leah took a bath that didn't calm her. Belting a robe around her waist, she walked up and down the hall, wringing her hands.

To hell with it. She had to talk to him.

Rushing back to her bedroom, she threw off the robe and rifled through her underwear drawer, choosing a black lace bra and matching panties. She'd never had the opportunity to wear the set before. It wasn't a good idea to wear it now.

She was tempting fate, for sure.

Ignoring her niggling conscience, she put on the lingerie, along with a pair of low-rise jeans and a slinky, scoop-necked top. It was New Year's Eve. If a woman couldn't dress sexy on an adult holiday, when could she?

She applied a touch of eye makeup and shimmery lip gloss, throwing caution to the wind. Slipping into ballet flats, she fluffed her damp hair, which had been dyed several shades darker than her natural honey-blonde.

Preparing food was therapeutic for her, so she made a plate of snacks to fit the occasion. Cheese, crackers, olives.

That done, she headed out the door, cutting across the lawn to Brian's house before she could change her mind.

She raised her hand to knock on the screen door. He was standing at the kitchen counter, frowning at a stack of papers. Building plans, she supposed. His features were illuminated by the glow of an overhead lamp.

He turned his head at the sound of her arrival, his dark brows lifting in surprise. Abandoning his plans, he strode toward her, opening the door. His eyes skimmed down her body in a slow visual caress. "Leah."

"I'm sorry," she said, her stomach fluttering. "I overreacted. I do that a lot."

He leaned against the doorjamb, smiling easily. "It's okay. I kind of like that about you."

"You're kidding."

"No. It's better to overreact than not care about anything."

He was being kind—and she appreciated it. "The girls are sleeping and I can't leave them alone for long. Would you like to come over?"

His gaze darkened. "Yes."

"Just to talk," she blurted.

With a low laugh, he nodded. "I'll be there in a minute."

She stepped away from the front door, careful not to trip on the uneven sidewalk. "See you then."

While she waited for him to join her, she tidied up the kitchen and set the cheese plate on the coffee table.

Although it was an evening for spirits, she didn't have any alcohol in the house, not even cooking wine.

Luckily, Brian brought his own. He arrived on her doorstep with two bottles of beer. "Is this all right?"

"Perfect," she said, waving him in and locking up behind him. She went to the kitchen, grabbing the bottle opener from the silverware drawer. He did the honors for them both, acting the gentleman.

"Cheers," he said, clinking his bottle against hers.

Leah followed his lead, taking a small sip. Normally she would have poured her beer into a glass but she didn't want him to think she was a snob. She was afraid she'd already given him that impression.

"Have a seat," she said, leading him to the couch. "I made some snacks."

He sat down beside her, glancing at the cheese plate. The reminder that she'd refused his dinner invitation hung in the air between them.

She cleared her throat. "I wanted to explain myself."

"You don't have to."

Taking another sip, she set aside her beer. "I'm sorry I accused you of lying. You didn't do anything wrong. It's just that John used to take us out to dinner a lot, even when we were drowning in debt. He hid the truth about our finances and pretended everything was fine until it was too late."

He was quiet for a moment. "I don't like being compared to your husband."

Leah cringed, thrusting her hands in her hair. "I'm not saying this right. I think I connected to the two situations in my mind, and judged you unfairly based on his mistakes. Does that make sense?"

He gave her an assessing look. "Yes."

"I'm sorry if I offended you. I guess I have…trust issues."

"I understand."

"Do you?"

"Of course. You think I don't have issues, after the childhood I had? You trigger some of my old wounds, too."

"What do you mean?"

"Well, the fact that you hold yourself at a distance kind of messes with my head. Every time I get close, you back away. On the one hand, you're sexy and mysterious, and I'm a normal guy who likes the chase. But deep down I'm still that scrawny foster kid who felt abandoned and unwanted."

Heat rose to her cheeks and tears filled her eyes. She looked away, embarrassed by the way his words affected her. He'd touched her on so many levels.

"What's wrong?" he asked, cupping her face.

She closed her eyes, letting the tears fall. His openness was like a balm to her soul. John had never shared his emotions with her. "I'm sorry I made you feel bad."

"You're not responsible for my upbringing, Leah."

"Thank you for telling me about it."

He brushed moisture from her cheek. "Thank you for listening."

She felt herself drifting toward him and paused. It wasn't fair to keep leading him on, but he was so hard to resist. "Why don't you have a girlfriend?" she asked, moving back a few inches and reaching for her drink.

He tore his gaze from her mouth. "I haven't dated anyone in a while."

"How come?"

"My last girlfriend and I broke up right after my sister died."

"Oh," Leah breathed, putting her hand on her chest. "That's terrible."

"Yeah." His expression was contemplative. "I think it was more my fault that hers."

"Why?"

"Talking about my childhood seemed to make her uncomfortable, so I didn't bring it up. She had a great family and couldn't really relate. But I liked her, and we got serious fast. She mentioned wanting kids."

"Did you?"

"Yes, but I had serious reservations about it."

"Most thoughtful people do."

"Mine are different than most."

"Why is that?"

"Well, I like kids, obviously, and I think I'd enjoy being a parent. But I don't know who my father is."

"Your mom never told you?"

"No. There were probably a number of possibilities."

She rested her head on his shoulder, her heart breaking for him. "That doesn't mean you wouldn't be a great dad."

"True, but I don't know what genes I'd be passing on, or even who I'm related to."

"Can you get your DNA checked?"

"Yeah. I was considering it when Brenda got in the car accident." He rubbed a hand over his mouth, as if disturbed by the memory. "I'd made a mistake in downplaying my past. Cassie knew I didn't have a father, but she wasn't clear on the details. When she met my mother at the funeral, she was horrified."

Leah smoothed her palm across his back, comforting him.

"I told her the ugly truth about my childhood and

she stopped talking about kids. It was over pretty soon after that."

Her loss, she thought. "You were right to be honest with her."

"I can't blame her for wanting out."

She massaged his upper arm, marveling at his strength, inside and out. He'd overcome a series of traumatic experiences and made a comfortable life for himself. "Hard times can either bring people closer or tear them apart. I wish John would have shared his troubles with me. I'd have welcomed it."

He glanced at her hand, frowning a little. "I'm sorry I got defensive earlier. I was trying to be up front with you about my past because I'd been burned before. Maybe I overcompensated by emphasizing the bad stuff. I didn't even realize I was doing it."

She set aside her beer bottle. "There's nothing to be sorry about. Your past doesn't bother me, although it makes me sad. I'm amazed by how well you've done. You're strong. Indestructible."

The corner of his mouth tipped up. "Hardly."

"Tough, then."

"In your hands, I'm putty."

She squeezed his firm biceps. "I don't think so."

His eyes glinted with heat, reminding her of their steamy embrace this afternoon. His body was more like marble than putty. He inched closer, sliding his arm between her and the couch. When his fingertips made contact with the exposed strip of skin above her low-rise jeans, her lips parted in surprise.

He used that opportunity to cover her mouth with his and kiss her soundly. In the pool he'd been tender and tentative, making sure she didn't panic. Tonight he showed no hesitation. Thrusting his tongue inside her mouth, he slipped his hand lower, feeling the lacy edge of her thong panties.

She moaned, twining her tongue around his. Her sexy lingerie revealed more than skin; it suggested that she'd thought about making love to him, and had dressed accordingly.

With a low growl of approval, he pressed her into the couch cushions, deepening the kiss. When her breasts met the hard wall of his chest, they swelled against the cups of her bra, nipples tightening. Heat spiraled between her legs.

Panting with excitement, she explored the bunched muscles in his shoulders, kissing him harder. He broke contact with a frown, seeming annoyed by the layers between them. She yanked her shirt over her head and watched his eyes glaze over. Her nipples were clearly visible beneath the delicate black lace.

He stretched out on top of her, trailing his lips down her throat. She thrust her hands in his hair, encouraging him. Pushing aside the fabric of her bra, he closed his mouth over her puckered nipple, laving the rosy tip.

"Oh," she breathed, drowning in pleasure. When he stopped suddenly, she felt a sharp pang of dissatisfaction.

"Your phone is ringing."

The sound registered, a low-pitched trill. Leah scrambled out from underneath him, tugging her bra into place. "I'm sorry, I—have to answer it."

He made no protest as she held her shirt to her chest and rushed into the kitchen. Glancing at her daughters' bedroom door, which was still closed, she picked up the cordless and murmured a shaky hello.

"Miss Hansen? This is Deputy Marshal Dominguez."

Chapter 7

Leah's stomach dropped at the sound of his voice.

She turned her back on Brian. "What is it?"

"We've been investigating the matter at Green Market and an issue has been brought to our attention. The owner has loose ties to the same criminal organization as Mariano Felix. There is a possibility that he reported seeing you to Felix, who came in himself to make a positive identification."

"Oh, my God," she said, her mind reeling. "It was really him."

"We're looking into it. The owner is on a business trip, unavailable for questioning, which is also suspicious."

"What should I do?"

"For now, we're asking you to sit tight. The good news is that Felix probably doesn't know where you live. If he was indeed targeting you, the fact that you spotted him screwed up his plans. He wasn't able to harm you or follow you. By contacting us, you did exactly what witnesses are supposed to do in this situation."

She glanced over her shoulder, where Brian was waiting patiently, a curious expression on his face. "I don't want to move again."

"If we catch him, you won't have to."

Leah took a deep breath, pain spearing through her chest. She couldn't do this anymore. The stress was destroying her.

"We're starting twenty-four hour surveillance on your residence. There will be an undercover deputy marshal stationed in front of the house until the issue is resolved. You need to stay inside tonight. Is that clear?"

"Of course," she said, biting her lower lip. "I have a guest right now."

"Who?"

"My next-door neighbor."

"Brian Cosgrove?"

"Yes."

"Ah. He checks out."

"You've investigated him?" she whispered.

"Just a basic background report. No prior arrests. Let us know when he leaves so we can notify the undercover unit."

Her cheeks heated with embarrassment. The first time she'd entertained a man since her husband's death, and she'd been caught by a team of deputies. After exchanging a few more details with Dominguez, she hung up.

Brian obviously wanted to know who'd called. Instead of asking, he waited for her to offer the information. She put her shirt on, walking back to the living room. The Felix update had been like a splash of cold water.

Sitting down beside Brian, she took a hard swig of beer, wiping her mouth. When she hazarded a glance at him, he was studying her. "I have something to tell you."

"What?"

She twisted her hands in her lap. Disclosing information about the Federal Witness Protection Program was strictly prohibited. If she had to be relocated, he couldn't go with her. Only close family members, such as spouses and children, were allowed in the Program. "I might have to move."

"Why?"

She hesitated.

"Is your husband alive? Is he after you?"

"No, he's definitely dead. I...I watched him get executed."

His eyes widened with concern. "When?"

"A little over a year ago." She moistened her lips, preparing to disclose all. Brian was a good person, and he deserved an explanation. She couldn't bear to let him think she would toy with him or abandon him. "I walked in on him and his killer."

Brian swore under his breath, raking a hand through his hair.

Holding back her tears, she told the whole story, careful not to mention any specific names or places. "I've already been relocated once."

Understanding dawned. "Are you a federal witness?"

She looked away. "I can't answer that."

"Why would they move you again?"

"I saw him at the market yesterday."

"The killer?"

She nodded, her throat closing up.

"Did he try to hurt you?"

"No. I think he meant to follow me home."

"My God. No wonder you were upset."

"I wasn't sure it was him. Apparently, they have reason to believe it was." Trying to stay calm, she forced herself to continue. "There's a deputy parked outside. He knows you're here with me. I'll understand if you want to leave."

His brows rose in surprise. "You want me to stay?"

"Yes," she said, laying her heart on the line. "But I can't make any promises. I might have to disappear tomorrow, and that's not fair to you."

"It doesn't sound fair to you, either."

"I chose this life."

"Did you have another option?"

Fresh tears rose to the surface, threatening to rush over. "I'm sorry. I knew I couldn't get involved with anyone. I shouldn't have led you on."

"You didn't lead me on," he said, seeming angry. "I'm the one who dressed like Santa Claus and knocked on your door. I could tell you weren't interested in a relationship, but I couldn't leave it alone. I couldn't leave you alone." He gave her a naked look, pain etched on his face. "I think I'm falling in love with you, Leah."

His confession stole her breath away. "You're what?"

"I'm falling in love with you. Seeing you and the girls at my house filled this empty place inside me. I've been renting the place out since my sister died, working round the clock on these crappy remodels. Avoiding people. And then you came along, and I couldn't stay away." He reached out to take her hand. "I've never felt like this before."

Leah blinked back her tears. Although they might

make a very happy family, she couldn't allow herself to imagine a future with him. He belonged in that house by the ocean—and she didn't belong anywhere.

"I don't care if we have one week together, one night or one hour. I want to be with you." He pressed his lips to her cheek. "I want to touch you," he said in her ear, brushing aside her hair to kiss her neck.

The heat they'd generated a few minutes ago sparked back up in an instant. She tilted her head to the side, giving him greater access. "Let's go to the bedroom," she whispered, needing to feel his naked skin against hers.

His mouth froze on her neck. "Are you sure?"

In response, she rose to her feet, holding her hand out to him. When he took it, she laced her fingers through his and led him to her room. The ceiling fan in the hall whirred lazily. It absorbed soft sounds, but didn't prevent her from hearing the children, who sometimes woke in the middle of the night.

She locked the bedroom door, just in case. When she reached out to turn off the lamp, he stilled her hand. "Leave it on."

A thrill raced down her spine. She tugged her blouse over her head, enjoying the feel of his eyes on her. He returned the favor, removing his T-shirt. His jaw flexed as she studied his well-muscled torso. Swallowing hard, she unsnapped her jeans and pushed them down her hips. The peekaboo lace panties revealed as much as her bra.

Brian's gaze trailed over her pert nipples and down her belly, settling on the triangle between her legs. His throat worked convulsively.

Leah closed the distance between them, pressing her lips to the center of his chest. He lifted his hand to the back of her head, mussing her hair. His erection throbbed against her stomach and his heart beat a sexy tattoo against her cheek. She shivered, struck by a powerful urge to drive him wild.

If this was the only night they had, she'd like to make it memorable.

Sinking to her knees on the carpet, she dragged her open mouth down his taut belly, nipping his skin. He groaned a faint protest, tightening his hand in her hair. She unfastened the buttons on his fly and molded her palm around his erection, stroking him through the stiff denim. Her eyes widened as she explored his entire length.

She glanced up at him, moistening her lips.

With a strangled growl, he lifted her to her feet and crushed his mouth over hers. His tongue plunged in and out, mimicking the act she'd meant to perform. She moaned in pleasure, wanting him to use her body the same way.

They fell back on the mattress. His lips never left hers as he climbed on top of her, hands roving her curves. He fit his erection into the notch of her thighs and cupped her bottom, thrusting against her.

Leah gasped into his mouth, her senses rioting. She couldn't remember the last time sex had felt this good.

Nothing had ever felt this good.

"Please," she said, gripping the muscles in his back. She pushed down his boxer shorts and dug her nails into his taut buttocks.

He paused, breathing hard against her neck. "Wait."

"Why?"

"If I'm not careful, this will be over too soon." Rolling to one side, he skimmed his hands along her rib cage, setting a slower pace.

She unhooked her bra.

He tossed aside the wisp of underwire and fabric, covering her bare breast with one hand. When he brushed his thumb over the ripe tip, she shuddered. "Too rough?" he asked, lifting his gaze to her face.

She realized that he'd taken her earlier words to heart. "I love the way your hands feel," she said, arching into his palm. His calluses made a sharp contrast to her soft, sensitive skin. The textured surface rubbed across her tender nipples, abrading her sweetly. "Touch me everywhere."

Taking the hint, he slipped his hand into her panties. When he found her hot and wet, he gritted his teeth. She spread her legs wide, begging for more. His finger dipped inside obligingly, sinking deep.

"Like this?"

"Yes."

He slid his finger in and out, kissing her parted lips. Then he removed his slick fingertips from her panties and circled her tight nipples, making them glisten. She moaned at the sight, her breasts quivering. When he lowered his head to lick the rosy tips, she couldn't take it anymore. "Brian, please."

He put his hand back into her panties. Instead of penetrating her, he caressed the taut nub of her arousal, strumming back and forth. The stimulation was exquisite. She began to shake, seconds from exploding. But, before she could reach climax, he stopped.

"I have to taste you," he said, stripping her panties away from her throbbing flesh. Leah was too far gone to feel embarrassed when he settled between her legs, admiring the little triangle of honey-blond hair. "Very pretty."

She squirmed as he parted her with his fingertips,

exposing her swollen sex. Giving her a hungry look, he closed his mouth around her, sucking gently. Seconds later, she shattered, biting the edge of her fist to keep from crying out.

When she opened her eyes, he was kicking off his pants, stretching a condom over his jutting erection. She kept her legs relaxed and open, her stomach fluttering with anticipation. His gaze caressed her tingling flesh once more before he stretched out on top of her, placing the tip of his erection where his mouth had been. "You're so sexy," he rasped, easing inside her, inch by inch. "Delicious."

With a low groan, he sank to the hilt.

Leah sucked in a sharp breath, clinging to his neck. She was very wet, and had no trouble adjusting to his size. After a brief pause, he began to move in and out, taking her to a new level of pleasure.

She wrapped her legs around his lean hips. Although he wasn't hurried or rough, he didn't hold back on the intensity. He rocked her against the mattress, slow and hard and deep. Each thrust brought her closer to ecstasy. She raked her nails down his smooth chest and over his clenched abs, panting for completion.

He buried himself in her, framing her head with his hands. "I can't last."

She groaned, almost there.

"Come," he said, pressing his pubic bone against her mound, moving in tight circles. "Come for me."

After one last nudge, she fell apart in his arms. He covered her mouth with his and kissed her passionately, swallowing her cries. His body shook against hers, hips jerking as he found his own release.

They clung together for a long time, hearts pounding, limbs entwined.

* * *

Brian touched his lips to Leah's naked shoulder, trailing his fingertips down her spine.

He'd been watching her sleep for over an hour. They'd stayed up most of the night, making love again and again. Although she'd been a willing participant—to say the least—he was mildly ashamed of himself for wearing her out. Soon, she'd have to get up and take care of her kids.

He'd never known a woman like her. His last girlfriend had been smart and pretty, with a nice personality, but their relationship had lacked depth, in comparison. They hadn't shared tearful conversations or searing kisses. He'd certainly never exhausted her in bed. With Leah, he felt *alive* again. He couldn't get enough of her.

The thought of losing her made his gut twist with despair. She could disappear from his life at any moment. He might not be able to endure the loss.

His hand stilled on her back, midstroke.

"Have you talked to your nieces?" she murmured, startling him. He hadn't realized she was awake. "Since they moved away, I mean."

"I called them on Christmas."

"So they know who you are?"

"They know I'm Uncle Brian."

She rolled over, distracting him with a view of her bare breasts. "You should make arrangements with their father. Schedule a visit."

He'd considered asking, but his stilted conversations with Peter hadn't encouraged him. Brian held a grudge against his brother-in-law for taking the girls to Boston and remarrying less than a year after his sister's death.

Peter had even requested that Brian not mention Brenda in phone calls, which rankled pretty hard.

"I can't forgive him for letting his daughters forget her."

She snuggled into the crook of his arm, rubbing her cheek against his biceps. "Maybe he'll reconsider when they're older. Speaking from the perspective of the surviving spouse, I know how hard it is to get through each day. I'm sure he had his hands full with twins. His decision might have been based on desperation." Kissing his chest, she added, "Besides, you don't have to like him to love those girls."

"I'll think about it," he said, knowing she was right. "But he might say no."

"He might say yes."

Brian pressed his lips to the top of her head. He'd do anything to please her, and he wanted to see his nieces. Mending the way with Peter would be worth it. "Are you bringing this up in case you have to leave?"

"I don't want you to be alone."

He smoothed a hand over her hair, enjoying the sexy disarray he'd caused. "I'm more worried about you."

She shifted beside him, aligning her lips to his. When her tongue slipped into his mouth and her thigh slid across his, he thickened with arousal, his body roaring back to life. After the night they'd had, he doubted he could perform again.

"You're killing me," she groaned. "How old are you?"

"Thirty-six. Too old for another round."

"Hmm. All evidence points to the contrary."

"That's just for show. If I tried to get on top of you, it would flee in protest."

She smiled, falling onto her back. "My parts would also protest."

"Are you sore? I'll kiss you better." He ducked under the covers, wrestling with her playfully while she dissolved in giggles. Although they didn't make love again, he felt satisfied. Just hearing her laugh filled him with happiness.

"I should go before your girls wake up," he said finally.

"Yes."

He put on his clothes from the night before while she donned a pair of soft pajama pants and a T-shirt with a cupcake on the front. After she called to let the deputy know he was leaving, she saw him outside. It was a cool, gray dawn, the sky bleeding with drizzle. The foggy marine layer would burn off in the midday sun.

He turned to kiss Leah goodbye. "I love you."

She hugged him hard. "I love you, too."

Brian hadn't expected her to say it back. In his experience, love didn't come easy, so the words touched him deeply, reaching a place no one else had. He felt like he'd been given the greatest gift of his life.

"I'll call you later," she said, smiling.

His throat closed up and he could only nod in response. Afraid to make a fool of himself by crying on her lawn, he walked the short distance to his house. Last night, he hadn't bothered to lock the front door.

As soon as he stepped inside, he paid for the oversight. A man came rushing from the shadows, swinging a crowbar.

Chapter 8

Leah was too excited to sleep.

She put on a pot of coffee and made blueberry muffins from scratch, humming a cheery tune. Brian was in love with her! And she loved him back. Today she was going to enjoy the present and not think about the future.

It was New Year's Day. Her resolution was to start living again.

Soon the kitchen was fragrant with the smell of fresh-brewed coffee and warm blueberries. On impulse, she poured a cup for Brian and wrapped a few muffins in a napkin. She wanted to surprise him.

The fog wasn't so thick that she couldn't see the deputy parked outside. He was very incognito, and if she hadn't been told what his car looked like, she wouldn't have noticed him. With a slight nod in his direction, she dashed next door.

Standing on the front step, she peeked through the screen. "Brian?"

He didn't answer.

She was about to open the door and walk in when she noticed his feet sticking out from behind the kitchen counter. His boots were pointed up at the ceiling, as if he'd stretched out on the floor for a nap.

Growing uneasy, she called his name louder. No response.

Last week, she might have entered the house to find out what was wrong. She'd have assumed he'd fallen, not been struck.

After her close call at the market, she couldn't afford to take that chance. She retreated a few steps, intending to alert the undercover officer. Before she got the chance, a figure burst through the screen door, coming straight at her.

She screamed, stumbling backward. Although he was wearing a ski mask, she knew it was Mariano Felix. Acting on instinct, she dropped the muffins and threw the coffee mug at him, splashing hot liquid in his masked face.

He cursed, swiping at his eyes with a gloved hand.

Her chest seized when she saw the gun in his other hand. As she turned to run, the edge of her shoe caught on the uneven sidewalk and she fell to her knees, crying out. A bullet cut through the air above her head.

The deputy marshal exited his vehicle, his weapon drawn. He strode forward, shouting at Leah to stay down.

Felix took aim at the new target and fired twice in rapid succession. The sound was oddly muted but the odor of gunshot residue assaulted her senses. She watched in horror as the deputy marshal crumpled to the ground.

Felix advanced to finish him off.

Leah didn't stick around. She scrambled to her feet and headed the opposite direction, using the same strategy that had saved her the last time she'd tangled with Felix. She couldn't worry about the deputy marshal or wonder what had happened to Brian. In order to protect her children, she had to run away from them.

She sprinted down the street and turned left, toward the shore. On New Year's Day morning, The Strand was eerily quiet. A few stray partygoers staggered along the sidewalk, and a homeless man pushed a shopping cart through an empty parking lot.

The damp air mixed with the smells of last night's debauchery, creating a stomach-curling miasma of spilled beer and public toilets.

Her canvas tennis shoes slapped against the wet pavement in a rhythm that matched her thundering heartbeat. Heavier footsteps pounded behind her, proving that Felix had given chase. Leah didn't know where to go. He would follow her into a house or vehicle. There was no time to hide, no place to run.

High tide limited her options further. Big waves crashed against the rocks, warning her to stay back. The beach was under water, and the surf was far from gentle this morning. She'd reached the edge of the ocean. The end of the road.

Bullets peppered the sidewalk, spurring her into motion. Taking a deep breath, she leapt onto the jumbled rocks and dove headfirst into the pounding waves. The rush of icy water sent her into an instant panic. She was helpless to fight against the powerful current and breath-stealing cold. But a darker danger awaited her on the surface.

Saltwater filled her eyes and nose as she sank down, letting the waves drag her out.

Brian groaned as he regained consciousness.

A sound he'd never heard before, but recognized as a bullet fired using a silencer, sent a chill racing down his spine. He struggled to keep his eyes open, bracing his hands on the kitchen floor to orient himself.

Leah was in trouble.

His hair was sticky with blood, his head throbbing in agony.

Leah was in trouble.

There was another muted gunshot, followed by a faint scream. Brian dragged his body upright, clinging to the unfinished countertop. Swallowing his nausea and ignoring the dull pain in his head, he stumbled toward the front door.

Leah was in trouble.

A man in a black ski mask was standing over a body in the middle of the street, his gun drawn. Brian wasn't sure how he'd been injured, but he didn't have any trouble guessing who the bad guy was.

The man in the mask left the corpse on the ground and took off running. Brian wiped the blood from his eyes and searched his immediate surroundings for Leah. She wasn't in his field of vision. The screen door was bent, hanging off the hinges. A broken coffee mug and a trio of smashed muffins littered his front walk.

He frowned at those items, trying to make sense of them.

His brain finally kicked into gear and he staggered

outside, looking down the street. The masked man was chasing a small figure in the distance.

Leah.

Brian couldn't catch them on foot—not in his condition. But he might have a chance in his truck. Limping toward the driver's side, he opened the door and climbed behind the wheel, wiping blood from his forehead. He fumbled for the keys and started the engine. When it turned over, he stepped on the gas, praying he wasn't too late.

The masked man turned left at the corner, his outline dissolving in the morning fog. Brian drove as fast as he dared. Keeping the truck on the road was a challenge in itself. His vision swam in and out, breaking his concentration. As he hooked a shaky left, the road before him shifted, floating out to sea.

Brian blinked the blood from his eyes, trying to clear his head. He was hallucinating. The urge to slump over the wheel and sleep was hard to resist.

When the street rematerialized, he accelerated and tightened his hands on the wheel, as if he could hang on to reality by exerting pressure. They were almost at the beach. Would Leah have gone this direction?

Through the heavy fog, Brian saw a dark figure on the rock border between the street and the ocean. The surf was up. He stepped on the gas, charging down The Strand. The man on the rocks lifted both arms, aiming his gun at the crashing waves.

Leah was in the water, barely staying afloat.

"No!" Brian cried out, terrified for her. Even if he managed to get out of his truck and overpower her attacker, which was unlikely, he might not be able to save her. He could barely stand, let alone swim.

But Brian wasn't a quitter, and he had a weapon of

his own. His work truck might be old and beat-up, but it was a heavy, dangerous piece of equipment. Using the best tool he had, he picked up speed, bracing himself for a kamikaze crash.

Gritting his teeth, he drove full tilt into the jagged rocks. His front bumper took out the masked man at the knee, sending him flying through the air. Brian's head hit the steering wheel as the truck tumbled into the ocean.

Water rushed in the driver's-side window and everything went black.

Leah was drowning.

With every wave that broke over her head, she became weaker. Brian had taught her how to tread water in a calm swimming pool. Doing it in a tumultuous ocean, while bullets speared the surface all around her, was impossible.

She couldn't stay calm, or float or catch her breath. Her lungs were burning and her throat felt raw. The cold seeped into her bones, robbing her ability to think.

When a truck slammed into the rocks at the shore, she screamed, ducking under water once again. She resurfaced during a lull between waves, gasping for air. The saltwater felt buoyant, keeping her afloat. Leah's sobs of terror quieted as she realized that Felix was no longer shooting at her.

In fact, he was lying on the rocks, his neck twisted at an odd angle.

She took a ragged breath, studying the truck that had rolled into the ocean. Cosgrove Construction, its side read. Brian was alive!

Before the next wave came, she got a good look inside the cab. Seawater was pouring through the windows. He was behind the wheel, unmoving. Maybe unconscious. If she didn't save herself, and him, they'd both die.

Mandy's face flashed before her, quiet and thoughtful. She pictured Alyssa's big smile. *I love you, Mommy.*

Tears rushed to Leah's eyes as a new resolve steeled her. She was the only parent they had left; she had to keep fighting. Filling her lungs with oxygen, she dove under the waves, kicking wildly. It wasn't graceful, but she didn't drown. Pushing aside her fear, she focused on Brian, remembering the feel of his lips against hers. He'd breathed new life into her. Now she would do the same for him.

Using every ounce of strength she possessed, she propelled herself through the water, making her way toward the upended truck.

As soon as she reached the passenger side, she clung to it, panting from exertion. Brian was wedged inside, his torso under water. She screamed for help, waving her arms at two surfers in the distance. They weren't close enough to assist her.

Luckily, the front windshield was shattered, offering a way in—and out. Safety glass floated on the surf, clinging to her wet hair. Leah crawled inside the cab and grabbed his legs, heaving with all her might. Somehow, she pulled him out from behind the wheel, maneuvering his upper body to the surface. When she saw how blue his skin looked, a cry of agony wrenched from her throat.

Soon, the surfers came to her aid. Working together, they were able to move Brian through the damaged window. Sirens rang out in the distance as they struggled to keep his head above water. Leah pressed her lips to his and exhaled, trying to resuscitate him.

He was so cold.

The next few minutes passed in a blur. An ambulance and a squad of police cars arrived. Brian's body was taken from the water on a rescue stretcher and carried away. Leah wanted to go with him, but she was detained for questioning.

"My kids," she said, accepting a scratchy wool blanket from a female police officer. "I need to check on my kids."

"We'll send someone to your residence right now," the policewoman promised. "Can you identify the man on the rocks?"

"Mariano Felix," she said, glancing in his direction. Someone had lifted the ski mask, exposing his sightless eyes. Shivering, she draped the blanket around her shoulders. It was over. But instead of relieved, she felt numb.

"Can you explain what happened?"

Leah didn't know where to begin. Before she could collect her thoughts, a gray midsize sedan pulled up to the scene. Deputy Marshal Joel Dominguez got out of the car, showing his badge to the officers who had already responded.

Over the past eighteen months, Dominguez was one of the few people Leah had interacted with. He'd been assigned her case, and although they didn't have a close personal connection, he was a good man.

Like Brian, he'd bought her girls a Christmas present.

Seeing Dominguez's concerned face made her own crumple with sorrow. She let out a choked sob as he wrapped his arms around her. "Are my daughters okay?"

"They're fine."

Leah wept harder, unable to stop. It was as if a year

and a half of tension and fear came pouring out of her, onto him. He patted her back awkwardly, as uncomfortable with tears as most men. When she quieted, he released her. "What about Deputy Marshal Stevens?" she asked, looking up at him.

He shook his head, a muscle in his jaw flexing.

"Oh, my God," she whispered. "I'm so sorry."

"It wasn't your fault, Leah."

She hugged the wool blanket around her body, her stomach twisted in knots. A man had given his life to protect her. "Does he have a family?"

"He has…had a fiancé. No kids."

Another good man lost. Her throat tightened and she glanced out at the choppy gray ocean. A light drizzle began to fall again, soaking the slate-colored rocks. She couldn't handle any more death.

If Brian didn't make it, she'd be devastated.

Chapter 9

Leah was able to return home before the girls woke up.

While a team of crime scene investigators from the U.S. Marshals Service processed the evidence outside, she removed her wet clothes and stepped into the shower, letting the hot spray ease her overworked muscles.

When she got out, she dressed quickly and took a plate of blueberry muffins to her daughters' room. She drew the curtains closed, insulating them from the violence. For a few minutes she watched them sleep, her eyes wet. Then she covered Alyssa's face with kisses and ruffled Mandy's hair, telling them both to rise and shine.

After breakfast, she called Dominguez. She wanted to go to the hospital to be with Brian. As soon as he gave the okay for them to leave, she packed a bag with snacks and activities, hustling the girls out the door.

They noticed the police cars and CSI vans, of course.

"What happened, Mommy?" Mandy asked.

"Brian got hurt. We're going to visit him."

Leah knew she was taking a risk by allowing the girls to come with her. If Brian was seriously injured, her daughters would be upset. On the other hand, the hospital was a more appropriate place for children than a murder scene.

The staff at Tri-City Medical wouldn't release any information about Brian because Leah wasn't a relative. So she waited patiently in the lobby while Alyssa colored pictures and Mandy wrote a get-well card. Soon a woman in scrubs called her name.

"I'll be right back," she told the girls, walking the short distance to the front desk.

"Mrs. Cosgrove?"

"No, I'm Leah. Brian's...girlfriend."

The woman introduced herself as an E.R. doctor and updated her on Brian's condition. He'd sustained a concussion and needed five staples in his scalp. "The good news is that he had no fluid in his lungs."

"How can that be?"

"Well, he was probably unconscious before he went under, so that helped to reduce the amount of water he took in. Also, one of the body's natural defense mechanisms is for the larynx to block the airway. This reflex only works during the first few minutes of drowning. He's lucky someone got to him in time."

Blinking tears from her eyes, she glanced back at her children, who were still coloring. "He's really going to be okay?"

The doctor smiled. "Yes. If he doesn't show any serious symptoms from the concussion, he can go home this evening."

She grabbed a tissue, sniffling. "When can I see him?"

"As soon as he wakes up."

Leah thanked her and went back to the waiting area, her spirits soaring. She was alive, her children were fine and Brian was recovering. For the first time in years, she envisioned a happy, hopeful future.

Dabbing at her eyes with the tissue, she sat down between her daughters.

"Is Brian going to die?" Mandy asked.

"No," she said, giving her a hug. "He'll be just fine. But he's sleeping right now and we have to let him rest."

Alyssa held up a picture of waves and sunshine. "Do you think he'll like it?"

Leah kissed the top of her sweet head. "He'll love it."

Her cell phone rang a few minutes later. It was Dominguez, inquiring about Brian. "They think he'll be able to go home tonight," she said.

"About that…"

"Is it safe?"

"For him, yes. We'll keep his name out of the incident reports. As far as the press is concerned, a deputy marshal lost his life protecting a witness. Anyone who looks into the matter will assume that Stevens killed Felix."

"Good," she said, relieved.

"That means no hero medal for Cosgrove."

"He won't mind."

"It's in his best interest not to."

"What about me?"

"We're reassessing your need for protection. As far as we know, Felix was working on his own. His crime boss would never sanction a hit on an innocent woman.

With Felix gone, your level of endangerment is low. He's the only one you could have testified against, so there's no reason for another member to come after you."

"Why did he attack Brian?"

"He must have spotted Stevens and known he couldn't approach your house. So he set a trap to draw you out."

She closed her eyes, taking a shaky breath. "I almost fell for it."

"Most people would. Felix probably wanted Cosgrove to look hurt, not dead. Otherwise he'd have just shot him."

Leah couldn't bear to think about it. "What's next?"

"For now, I'm recommending your transitional placement in WITSEC. As soon as the threat against you is evaluated and cleared, you'll be released from the program. You can go home, Leah."

She moistened her lips. "What if I don't want to?"

"It's your choice. I don't see any problem with you staying in Oceanside, but not at your current residence."

They discussed a few more details before she hung up. If she left the program, Leah could see her mom again. The prospect was appealing, but not urgent. She'd like for her daughters to have relationships with their grandparents.

After lunch, Leah was called back to the reception desk. "Mr. Cosgrove is awake and asking for you."

Pulse pounding with excitement, she grabbed the girls and rushed down the hall, searching for his room. When she found it, she peeked inside. Brian was resting in a hospital bed, his head bandaged. Although he looked tired, he smiled when he saw her, his teeth flashing white against his swarthy complexion.

"I colored you a picture," Alyssa said.

"Yeah? Let's see it."

She gave him the sunny seascape. "I drew water 'cause I know you like it."

"I do like it," he said, seeming touched by her thoughtfulness. "Thank you. I'm going to save this."

Mandy stepped forward with her card shyly.

"Did you make something, too?"

She nodded, handing it to him.

He read the note out loud. "'Get well soon so we can swim at your pool again. Love, Mandy and Alyssa.'" When he glanced at Leah, his eyes twinkling with humor, her heart skipped a beat. "This is great. I feel better already."

Leah sat the girls down on the next bed over, which was empty, and turned on a public television program for them. *Sesame Street* wouldn't hold their attention long, after a quiet morning in the lobby, but it might grant her and Brian a few minutes of privacy. She returned to his side, squeezing his hand.

"I'm glad you're all right."

"Are *you* okay?" he asked, lowering his voice. "I can't remember anything except being afraid for you."

"You saved me," she said simply.

"That's strange. I thought that you saved *me*."

She smiled. "Whatever."

"Was there a man in a mask?"

"He's gone now."

The tension in his face eased and he leaned back against the pillows. "Good. Will you have to leave town?"

"No, but I can't live in the house on Surfrider."

"Move in with me. I don't have any more renters scheduled. I'd love to have you and the girls at my place."

She was tempted to accept the offer on the spot. "You might regret it. Alyssa thinks it's fun to have screaming contests."

"I'm serious."

Her daughters started fighting over the remote control, proving that they were capable of being noisy and combative. "So am I."

"Happy houses aren't quiet, Leah."

Before Brian, she'd never have considered moving in with a man she'd only known a short time. She hadn't thought it was possible to fall in love so quickly, either. But after what they'd been through, the number of days didn't seem important. She felt safe with him. She didn't want to wait to start over.

"I'll have to ask Mandy and Alyssa how they feel," she said.

He grinned, knowing that her daughters would move in with an ogre if he had a private swimming pool. "It'll work out. I promise."

She believed him. "I love you, Brian."

"I love you, too." He tugged on her wrist, bringing her mouth to his for a tender kiss. "This morning I thought I was going to lose you. Now I feel like the luckiest man in the world. I don't want to let you go."

Tears blurred her vision as she sank to her knees at his bedside, wrapping her arms around him. "I don't want to let you go, either." He'd barged into her house, dressed like Santa, but she'd ended up with the best present: him.

He stroked her hair and she rested her head on his chest, feeling blessed. She had a new love, a new life and a wonderful New Year to look forward to.

* * * * *

KIDNAPPED AT CHRISTMAS

Jennifer Morey

To my homey. I'm so glad you found me.
And a special thank you goes to Samantha—for always
finding something to do when I write.

Chapter 1

Chloe Bradford finished the mock-up of her latest Christmas card design. Animated, 3-D stockings hung from a white brick fireplace she'd painted. They had furry collars and cheery red-and-green patches, a lot more cheery than she felt. Setting that on top of the other pieces she'd done, she looked up at the darkened window above her desk. City lights twinkled, full of color three days from Christmas. It had been a few years since seeing them made her feel lonely. She almost couldn't look at them right now.

Checking the clock on her five-year-old computer, she stood. Time to go to her day job at the supermarket down the street. She pushed her cheap office chair under the desk and turned to face her purely functional, hand-me-down living room. She kept her desk in here rather than her bedroom so she wouldn't feel so quarantined. Her apartment was beyond small. It was an oversize closet. There was barely enough room in her bedroom for a queen-size bed. All she had out here was her desk, what may pass as a shabby chic sofa that pulled out into a bed, a TV, and her bistro table in the tiny dining area, just off her cubbyhole of a kitchen.

Home sweet home.

She slipped into her knee-length jacket and stuffed her wallet and keys into her pocket. She had a cell phone but left it home when she went to work. No one would be calling her tonight anyway. She had the late shift with the produce crew and all her friends had plans for Christmas. It was just going to be one of those years. She was stuck alone for Christmas. Top that off with her boyfriend breaking up with her on Thanksgiving and you have a real Scrooge for Christmas.

Stepping out into the bitter cold Chicago night, she saw her breath through a steady peppering of snow along 159th Street. Haphazardly hung Christmas lights blinked from a poorly maintained, single-story house across from her equally run down apartment building. Passing darkened houses, one of them vacant, and another apartment building, she made it to a more commercial section. Cars drove slow over the icy road. A creepy-looking guy walked by her from the opposite direction, carrying a bottle in a bag. The hookers were starting early, too. Across the street, with the flashing lights of a twenty-four-hour pawn shop in the background, a woman in a fake fur coat with boots up to her knees bent over a passenger car window.

Her ex-boyfriend hadn't liked coming over to her place most of the time. She'd gone to his. This wasn't the best neighborhood so she'd overlooked the prejudice. She supposed she should have paid more attention to that sign. She'd been too enamored with him, with the two of them as a couple. When he'd told her he loved her, she'd believed him. When they'd talked about marriage, she'd thought he was sincere. She was excited to start a family with him. Turns out he had other plans, though, and they included a girl he'd met where he worked. Another engineer like him. She had to give him credit for telling her, and for assuring her that he hadn't had an affair on her. He was attracted to this woman and wanted to see where it led. He hadn't slept with her or dated her while they were together, only talked to her and asked if she was interested in dating him.

She couldn't even be mad at him. He hadn't done anything wrong. He'd just discovered he didn't love her and she couldn't make him.

Passing a storefront with cheap tinsel and gaudy flashing lights, she felt a kinship with the display. That's how her life looked right now. Cheap and gaudy. But cheap and gaudy to some people was something beautiful to others. Chloe saw herself that way. She may appear to live cheap and gaudy, but on the inside she was the Grand Canyon. A grand landscape of color and depth. She just wished someone other than herself could see that. Namely, a man.

Next door, someone opened the door to the Streetside Bar. Voices and music from the throng within drifted out into the street. She'd spent a few nights in there after Thanksgiving. Luckily, the survivor in her had pulled her through that phase. Cigarette smoke from three men standing outside floated by her. She ignored them as she passed, feeling them watch her but not afraid. She'd had run-ins with men like that before. They appeared tough but really they were misguided thugs who needed to be shown not everyone could be bullied. She'd made an example out of a couple of them. They knew to leave her alone.

At the corner she waited for the light and then crossed, walking toward the lights in the busy parking lot of Lawrence Tucker's, the supermarket that paid her paltry rent. Shopping carts were strewn all over the snow and ice-covered lot.

Chloe made her way inside, saying hi to coworkers on her way to the back. George looked at her funny. He managed the bakery.

After putting her coat away in her locker, she turned and saw her manager standing in the doorway, a grim look on her face. *Oh, great. Not again.*

"A customer returned some tomatoes earlier today," she said.

In a flash, Chloe remembered being interrupted when she was changing out the old tomatoes with new ones. Ever since the breakup she'd been doing that a lot at work.

"I'm sorry. Someone asked me where the marsala was and I showed them. I must have gotten sidetracked."

"It's happened too many times lately."

"I'm just going through a hard time right now, that's all."

Her manager shook her head and sighed with resignation. "I know it's almost Christmas, but this is out of my hands now. The customer claims to have gotten sick from one of the tomatoes. My boss told me to fire you."

A shock wave of disbelief rushed over her. "What?"

"I have to fire you, Chloe. I don't want to. I like you. So does everyone else, but..."

"Your boss told you to fire me. Right." Chloe took her coat back out of her locker and slipped it on again.

All the while the image of the homeless man carrying a bagged bottle of booze haunted her. She wouldn't make it through the next month.

"I did manage to get you a severance package. It isn't much, but I hope it will get you by until you file for unemployment and start receiving benefits."

Relief eased her anxiety. She faced her now ex-boss. First an ex-boyfriend, now an ex-boss, who handed her a manila envelope.

Chloe took it. "Thank you, Shirley. I'm sure whatever is in the severance package will help."

Her ex-boss's regret was palpable, a small consolation. "If there's anything I can do, just call. I'll give you a good reference if you need one. Don't worry about that."

"Thanks. Take care." Retracing her steps to the front, she waved to George and he somberly waved back.

Outside, she stopped and watched her breath through the falling snow. Going back home filled her with dread. She didn't want to be alone for Christmas. She was tired of being alone. Maybe her ex-boyfriend's rejection made her more aware of that. She could tell herself she was fine on her own, but the truth was she missed being part of a family. She'd gotten her first real taste of it with her ex-boyfriend, and when he left, he'd taken them away with him.

Maybe she'd take all her money, pack some essentials and get on a bus to anywhere but here. Move. Start over somewhere new. Somewhere prettier than Chicago.

What did she have to lose?

Mason Jaffee got out of his Charger and started toward the entrance of Lawrence Tucker's supermarket. A few spaces over, another man got out of his car at the same time. A quick glance had Mason stopping in his tracks. Axel Grant lit a cigarette as he approached. Not a tall man, or a big one, Axel still managed to appear menacing with his shaved head, thin black mustache and light gray eyes that had a desensitized look to them. He had always been distrustful of Mason, but this seemed out of the ordinary. Had he followed him here? Not good. Mason wasn't supposed to be seen tonight. Axel and his criminal friends thought he'd be gone by now. Knowing a raid was planned for New Year's Eve and his undercover work would finally be over, he'd made his excuses early. He couldn't wait to get out of Chicago.

"Hey, man. What are you doing here?" Mason asked. This could ruin everything.

He blew a stream of smoke into the cold air. "I was just about to ask you the same thing, *Michael*."

The way Axel said his false name made him wary. He caught sight of a woman walking toward them, bundled up in a brown coat that came to her knees and a hat that kept her hair pressed to her head.

"You said you were going to Florida for Christmas," Axel said.

"I am. I was just delayed."

"Uh huh." He took a drag on his cigarette. "What delayed you?"

The woman drew closer, noticing them now.

This was a bad time to be caught in a lie. Why was Axel here? He had to come up with a convincing answer to his question. Quick.

Acting on impulse, he slipped his arm around the woman as she was about to pass and drew her close to him. "Hey, baby. Sorry I'm late." Feeling her resist, he caught sight of a Lawrence Tucker's name tag peeking through her partially open jacket and looked at Axel. "Chloe had to work tonight. We're leaving to spend Christmas with my sister the day after tomorrow."

He prayed the woman would play along for a little while. Right now she stared up at him with a blank look, the manila envelope she held smashed between them. She was about six inches shy of his six-two frame and fit against him nicely.

Axel stared at the woman before turning to Mason. "I never understood why Donovan liked you. If it were up to me, I'd have gotten rid of you a long time ago." He parted his leather jacket to reveal his gun.

Chloe inhaled a sharp breath.

"She really your girl?" Axel gave Mason a drilling look.

"Yeah, man. Just met her a month ago. She got called into work tonight, right, baby?"

Numbly, the woman nodded. Good, she was at least street smart. Living in this neighborhood, you had to be.

"Marcus said he saw you at the gas station earlier today. I stopped by your place to see what you were still doing here and followed you here." Axel glanced over at Chloe. "He didn't mention a woman."

"Chloe wasn't with me this morning."

Axel took another drag off his cigarette, his obvious suspicion unnerving. "Why are you keeping her a secret?"

"I didn't know my girlfriends were part of the business."

With hard, emotionless eyes, Axel contemplated him a moment, blowing smoke out. Mason couldn't tell if he'd decided to believe him or not.

"You and Frankie are good friends," he finally said. "Ain't that right?"

Frankie. Tanner Sullivan. He was the other agent who'd been working undercover with him. Why was Axel bringing him up now? His bad feeling got bigger.

"I know him." Mason wouldn't make the stretch and call them good friends, but they did work together.

"Did you know he was a fed?"

Was. Mason feigned surprise while the magnitude of that sank in. They knew Tanner was an agent. "Frankie was FBI? You sure?"

"Yeah, I'm sure." Another eerie moment of contemplation passed. "You a fed, too, *Michael?*"

Mason gave out a grunt of false cynicism. "That's funny, Axel. You got any more jokes for me tonight?"

"You see me laughing?"

Why was Axel asking if he was an agent? Why play cat and mouse? Why not come right out and say he knew he was a fed. Maybe because he didn't know. Mason hoped that was the case. He hoped Tanner hadn't talked. Not so close to the raid.

"How'd you find out?"

"Heard him talking to his wife. Frankie told us he wasn't married. We found his badge when we stopped by to ask him about his mysterious phone calls. But even that wasn't enough to make him talk."

They'd bugged his phone? How had Tanner missed that? Mason checked his apartment every day and only used his FBI-issued cell phone for correspondence with anyone outside his undercover work, and he was always careful about when and where he made the call.

"He wouldn't say why he was here?"

"No."

"Where is he now?"

Axel drew on his cigarette again and then blew out, watching Mason closely. "Feeding the fish in the Chicago River by now."

They'd killed him. Mason stamped down his exploding fury. So close to the raid, Tanner got caught. "Problem solved, then."

"Maybe."

Mason didn't respond. Axel was only taunting him. He wouldn't have said anything if he fully believed he was an agent. His conundrum stemmed from his jealousy over Mason's relationship with Donovan. As long as Mason was careful, he could still pull off this investigation. And now that Tanner was dead, he had more motivation than ever to take every single one of these sleazy bastards down.

Axel's gaze drifted over Chloe and then back to Mason. "Bring her to Donovan's tomorrow night. He's going to want to meet her...and talk to you about Frankie. Now that your trip was delayed, that shouldn't be too much of a problem...right, *Michael?*"

Why would Donovan want to talk to him about Frankie? Because they'd appeared to be friends? Or was he beginning to listen to Axel?

Mason nodded, glancing at the woman he didn't know. "Yeah, sure. We can manage that. You don't have to work tomorrow night, do you, baby?"

Chloe shook her head.

Tossing his cigarette to the ground, Axel took in the exchange. "If she ain't your girlfriend and I find out you've been lying to us, you're a dead man...and so is she. You follow me?"

"Merry Christmas to you, too." Mason turned, guiding Chloe to the blue Charger the agency had leased for him. "Get in." And then quieter, "Please."

She met his eyes and hesitated. Glancing fearfully back at Axel, she got into the passenger side.

"See you at the party," Axel said.

Mason ignored him and got into the car himself, shutting the door. Seeing Axel get back into his own car, he swore.

"What the hell was that all about?" Chloe asked.

"I'm sorry. Really. I didn't know what else to do. I'm not supposed to be here right now. But he saw me." Dragging his hand through his dark hair that needed a cut, he drove out of the parking lot. Tanner was dead. How much did he actually reveal? Would he be walking into a trap tomorrow night?

"I live just up the street," Chloe interrupted his thoughts. "Take me there and we can forget this ever happened."

She wasn't even afraid of him, he noticed. She'd been afraid of Axel, but Axel had a gun. He marveled over that, taking her in askance. She did live in this awful neighborhood.

"I can't risk that," he finally said.

Axel would make sure Donovan sent someone to spy on her. They might even kidnap her and force her to *work* for them once they discovered she wasn't really his girlfriend.

He felt Chloe staring at him, ready to go up against him. He had to admire her for that, for her toughness. And yet...she had this air of femininity about her.

"Open the glove box. I have a badge in there. I'm an agent for the FBI. I'm here on assignment. I've been working undercover to bring down a prostitution operation that forces unwilling women to work for them."

Still, she just stared at him. But finally she reached for the glove box and opened it. Pulling out the wallet that held his badge, she opened that and began a careful scrutiny.

"You can call and check to see if it's legitimate," he said.

Folding the wallet, she put it back into the glove box and shut it. Then she sat there, staring straight ahead as if contemplating what to do.

"Just take me home, *Agent Jaffee.*" She told him the address.

Instead of agreeing, he used his phone to call his SAC. He'd work on her later.

Reid Richardson answered.

"Parker Street," Mason said. It was their code to let the SAC know who was calling and about which investigation.

"What happened?"

He must know something was wrong. Mason wouldn't have called otherwise. "It's Tanner. I had a run-in with Axel when he thought I was supposed to be in Florida." He explained what Axel had said.

Reid let loose a bevy of curses when he heard Tanner was dead.

"Don't send a swarm of agents to look for the body. Let the locals do the search. That way it doesn't look like I reported the crime. It could have been anyone who saw something."

"I want you out of there. Now. Your cover's been shaky ever since you started this. We'll proceed with the raid as planned."

"We need to move faster than that. Axel invited me and my new girlfriend to a party tomorrow night. They'll all be there. Move the raid up."

Reid was silent for a long time. "What do you mean your new girlfriend?"

"A woman helped me convince Axel I was legitimate. I should have been gone days ago, visiting family in Florida." He explained what happened in the parking lot. "Move up the raid."

"Is the woman agreeable? She going with you to the party?"

He glanced over at her and saw her watching him with street-smart calculation. "I don't know yet."

"She has to agree, Jaffee. And she's going to need protection either way. Whether it's you or someone I send, we have to make sure she's okay. You involved her."

"I know. I'll watch over her until we've got everyone. After the party she can go back to her life." He met her eyes to let her know he meant it. The soft blue of them narrowed back at him. It wasn't until then that he realized she had a really pretty face. She wore no makeup, but her features were striking. Strands of blond hair peeked out from under the hat. She had chin-length hair but it was thick. He couldn't tell what the rest of her looked like under the bulk of her coat.

"Let me know if you have trouble with that. Offer her some incentive if you need to."

"Thanks, Reid."

"And Jaffee."

"Yeah?"

"I want them, too. More now than ever. I'll let you know the details when I have them."

Nothing pissed off an agent more than losing one of their own. "I'll be waiting."

At Chloe's place, it would appear, since she wanted him to take her home.

They ended the call.

"Take me home," she demanded.

"I will…but I'm going to have to stay with you until this is over."

"Like hell you will."

"What do you think Axel will do if he finds out I lied?"

"*You* lied. This has nothing to do with me."

"It does now. They think you're my girlfriend. That was the Special Agent in Charge of this investigation. We were planning a raid on New Year's Eve, but this changes things. We're moving the raid to tomorrow night. At the party Axel will be expecting us to attend, remember?"

She stared at him again.

"I need you there with me or this won't work."

No response. What was going through her head?

"I'll be out of your hair before Christmas. Nothing should interfere with your holiday plans."

That made her blink slowly. "I don't have any holiday plans."

She didn't?

"Were you really going to go to Florida for Christmas?" she asked.

"No. I was going to go to Montana. My parents retired there. My entire family will be there for Christmas." Yet again, she stared at him. "Because it has to be a secret…you know…to maintain my cover. Florida, not Montana."

"Where in Montana?"

Why did she care? "Woodland. It's a small town just north of Flathead Lake. Remote as hell."

"Is it pretty?"

"Yeah. Beautiful. Nothing much there, though." Boring. Quiet. Cold.

"Take me with you," she all but blurted.

And it was his turn to stare at her. "To...you want to go with me to my family's house for Christmas?"

"Not to your family's house. Take me with you to Montana. Buy me a plane ticket. Just get me there."

That stopped him. Why did she want to go to Montana?

"I was fired tonight."

Right before Christmas? "That was awfully thoughtful of your boss."

"My mom died when I was sixteen and I lived with my stepfather until he tried to assault me one night. I left my senior year in high school, and I've been on my own ever since."

The way she explained such a tragic upbringing, so matter-of-factly, revealed her hardened exterior. "I'm sorry. But...why are you telling me this?"

"Some people have it easy. It's never been easy for me. Nothing's gone right for me here. So why not start completely over? I want to leave Chicago. I don't have much money, and what I do have I need to save so I can find a place to rent and get by until I find a job."

She wanted him to buy her a plane ticket and take her with him to Montana. "I don't know..."

"I'll go to the party with you, but only if you buy me a plane ticket to Montana."

"Deal. But I stay with you from now until we get there."

Her smile sparkled all over her face. "Deal."

Chapter 2

Chloe led Mason up the narrow, creaking stairs to her apartment door. Down the hall a baby cried and she could hear a woman talking to soothe it. From somewhere else, a television blared. Someone coughed. All the familiar sounds of home.

Mason closed the door behind him and looked around. His absorption made her more acutely aware of her modest dwelling than usual. While her lack of money was evident, she'd made attempts to turn a hovel into a home. She wondered if he noticed the artsy lampshade she'd picked up at a flea market, or the small glass vase with a single flower on the table.

Going into her bedroom, she removed her coat, covertly eyeing Mason. He removed his jacket and draped it over the arm of the sofa. Hanging her coat up in the tiny closet, she saw him wander over to the window in the living room. It had a pretty good view of the city.

Looking down, he saw the Christmas cards on her desk. He picked them up and leafed through them.

Something about seeing him do that pricked her. She didn't know why. Maybe it was too personal, maybe it mattered too much what he thought. He was a good-looking man, with dark hair and amazing green eyes and a hot body to go with them. Tall. Sexy in the green flannel shirt that brought attention to his eyes and dark jeans that flattered a tight butt and hinted to a manly shape in front. And he was an FBI agent. He had an exciting job. That made him even sexier to her. Annoyed by her attraction to a stranger who could have gotten her hurt or killed tonight, she went to him. Reaching around his side, she snatched the cards from him, stuffing them into a tote where she kept her small laptop.

"Sorry."

She lifted her head to look at him, caught for a second by the sound of his voice, and next, his glowing green eyes. Without saying anything, she went into the kitchen to throw together some cheese nachos.

A few minutes later, she emerged from the kitchen balancing two plates and a bowl. Seeing that he'd taken a seat on her shabby chic sofa, she handed him a plate of tortilla chips with melted cheese over them and put the bowl of salsa on the coffee table.

"Cheese nachos one of your specialties?" he asked.

Hearing his teasing tone, she sat beside him with her own plate. "Don't you like nachos?"

"Sure, if they have more toppings on them."

Dipping a cheesy chip into some salsa, she chewed and decided not to respond to that.

"A steak with a baked potato would have been better," he complained.

"Not on my budget."

"I could have gotten us something to eat."

"I like cheese nachos."

He dipped a chip and ate one, glancing around her apartment, probably thinking what a dump she lived in and no wonder why she couldn't afford more toppings on the nachos.

"What are you going to do with all your furniture?" he surprised her by asking.

In an instant she realized she didn't care all that much what happened to her things. There were some small items she wouldn't want to part with, but nothing that wouldn't fit into a suitcase. "I can't afford to store anything. I guess I'll just leave it here." Getting fired sure had turned a switch in her. The final straw. The only thing that mattered to her now was leaving this place behind. That's what made her want to do something crazy like pose as Mason's girlfriend and go with him to Montana.

"I'll pay for a unit," he said. "Cover you for a year. We can move it tomorrow." She watched him look around at her meager possessions again. "Shouldn't take too long."

She angled her head with her amazement. "You'd do that for me?"

"You help me, I help you."

"You're getting me out of this city. That's plenty."

"And you're going to be my girlfriend tomorrow night. It's the least I can do."

Did he think that was a hardship for her? She checked him out sitting beside her, sex appeal galore. Surely he didn't mean that. He must mean the danger. She'd risk her life by helping him. What if someone discovered he was an agent and she wasn't really his girlfriend?

Maybe propositioning him for a ticket out of Chicago

wasn't a very bright idea. Maybe he was getting more out of this deal than she was and that was why he felt compelled to pay for storing her things. So what if he was an agent and she'd seen his badge. Maybe she should have told him to get lost.

Even as the doubts came, everything inside her rebelled. Getting fired had pushed her to a precipice. Meeting Mason had been the catalyst that pushed her over the edge. There was no turning back now. The intensity of her resolve was unshakable. She simply did not want to live like this anymore. Tough on the outside because she had to be and yearning for a softer life on the inside. Mason was her way out.

"How old are you?"

The question took her aback. Why was he asking? "Twenty-seven."

"Did you go to college?"

"No." She munched on a chip.

"I'm thirty-two," he provided as though he'd expected her to ask.

"You probably went to college, too."

He looked over at her. "Have you ever thought of going freelance with your greeting cards?"

Was he asking these questions because he was interested or was he trying to figure out how she'd ended up here? "I've applied to some companies."

"You're really good, you know."

His compliment warmed her. She could tell he was sincere. "Thanks."

"What led you to work for Tucker's?"

"Starvation and the need for a roof over my head."

He grinned at her sarcasm. "And maybe an evil stepfather."

Recalling she'd mentioned her stepfather earlier,

Chloe understood where his curiosity stemmed. He wondered if that's why she ended up here. "Yes, he was evil. I bet my mother never knew he likes teenagers. He didn't get far with me, though. I fought him. Gave him a black eye. Needless to say, he didn't stop me from packing a suitcase and I haven't seen him since."

His eyes softened a fraction, getting the answer he was after. "And you've been fighting ever since."

"Yes, and it's time I stopped."

She saw him register the reason she was going with him to Montana. To her, leaving Chicago meant no more fighting. And he'd been interested enough to gently pry it out of her. If she had any remaining doubts about him, they were gone now. She could trust him to do as he agreed. Even more amazing, she couldn't recall ever feeling that way with anyone. Maybe because no one had ever helped her do anything so meaningful.

Noticing him staring at her, she saw the change in the way he looked at her. He studied her face as though absorbing it into his memory, her eyes, nose, lips. Lower. Physical interest. A spark of heat sprang from the energy between them. Chloe got caught up in it, in him, and sensed he'd fallen under the same spell.

"Are you seeing anyone?" he asked.

She smiled.

"Sorry. Forget I asked." He leaned back against the sofa.

"I was seeing someone," she answered anyway. And then the reminder pulled her mood down. "He broke it off on Thanksgiving so he could start seeing a woman with a college degree."

"Nice guy. You've had a rough holiday season so far."

"I thought he was the one for me."

He nodded as though familiar with that.

"Been there, have you?"

"After the third time, I gave up."

Three? "What did you do? Scare them off with your gun?"

He chuckled. "No."

"What made you decide to become an FBI agent, anyway? It's so dangerous, and…you can't be around much."

"My parents sent me to college, and being the young, aggressive guy I was, I went for something that wouldn't bore me after twenty years."

Definitely not boring. "How long have you been here? In Chicago, on assignment."

"A year."

"A *year?* Playing the role of a pimp?"

"Not a pimp. I was a guard, if you will. I watched the girls. Made sure no one hurt them."

Being used as a prostitute had to hurt enough. "Why didn't you help them escape?"

"I did help a couple of them. The bigger goal was to destroy the entire operation. Stop them from hurting any more women. I had to be careful."

"How do they force the women? I mean, I've heard a little about that on the news, but…"

"Mostly they find women in foreign countries who want to come to America. They smuggle them in and tell them they have to work to pay back the cost of their relocation. Sometimes they threaten to call Immigration."

Imagining what it would be like to be caught in that situation, Chloe turned away. "How awful."

"You have no idea."

After a while, she turned back to him. "It's good

what you do." Helping those women. Getting rid of those unscrupulous criminals. But it came with a cost, and she was beginning to understand why such a handsome man could have lost so many women. "No wonder why you've been dumped so many times."

He lifted his brow at her.

"Your job. You're never home. You pretend to be a criminal."

"Renee didn't leave me because of my job."

Renee. "Which one was Renee? One, Two, or Three?"

"Three." He was somber now. "I wouldn't ask her to marry me so she stopped waiting. She married Tanner instead, my partner on this assignment."

Chloe inhaled sharply along with her shock. "The one who was…"

"Yeah. Killed."

How did he feel about that? Losing his partner who married his ex-girlfriend? "Doesn't that bother you?" She shook her head. "I mean, that she married your partner. Of course you care that Tanner was killed." She paused. "Don't you?"

"He wasn't a close friend, but he was my partner. He didn't start seeing Renee until a year after our breakup."

He'd said he wouldn't marry her, but she sensed some anguish from him. "Did you love her?"

"Yes."

"Then why didn't you marry her?"

"I should have."

He should have.

It had been a long time since Chloe had worn a dress. Feeling as if she'd dressed for Mason wasn't helping. Neither did noticing how he'd taken the time to appreciate the finished product. He'd done that at her apartment and then in the car, and now she'd just caught him looking at her as they walked to a party like it was a date. Heat kept rising between them. And it was scalding now.

"If anyone asks, we met at Tucker's," he said.

She nodded.

"And my parents live in Orlando. They think we just met, so it's okay if you don't know much about me."

"Have we had sex yet?"

His head snapped toward her. "They'd believe it more if we have."

She was glad it was winter or she'd have broken out into a sweat by now.

Trying to divert her focus, she took in the flashing Christmas lights that flattered the roofline of the big fancy house. A gigantic Christmas tree glittered through an equally gigantic window. But it didn't dim her awareness of Mason. He looked like a fairy tale in a black suit and white shirt. His green eyes captivated her and he kept his thick black hair on the shaggy side. A little over six feet with broad shoulders, he was formidable. He also looked like he belonged in that suit. Unlike her, who felt more comfortable in jeans.

Mason didn't knock. He opened one of the doors and guided her in ahead of him. A throng of perhaps a hundred filled the main room, kitchen and library off the entry. A few peppered the upper level at the top of a curved and grand stairway. Christmas lights and garland wound around the banister and the enormous tree was stunning in the front window.

It seemed so odd to see people who forced women into prostitution so eloquently dressed. And it made her sick to know this big home was purchased with the money they brought in.

When Mason slipped his hand onto the small of her back, she stiffened along with a flash of warmth.

"Would you like something to drink?" he asked.

She thought about asking for a beer, but how would that look? She didn't see any women holding a beer. "Wine or champagne."

"Be right back."

She watched him go to one of the small, portable bars that were set up in the house and stand in a short line. A man at the top of the stairs caught her attention, and she saw him look from Mason to her and it felt more like scrutiny. Mason greeted another man who came to stand in line. The man smiled and exchanged what appeared to be amicable conversation, but someone else turned from the bar and eyed Mason suspiciously as he passed. Chloe glanced around the room and saw two other men watching Mason.

When he approached her with a glass of champagne and a drink for himself, she was captivated by the way he moved and the way he zeroed in on her. Sexy and definitely drool-worthy. His eyes still held hers as he handed her the glass. He sipped his drink and scanned the crowd. Chloe noticed the same men still eyeing them and began to wonder if they were in trouble.

"You look beautiful tonight," Mason said.

He was either good at covering his emotion or not worried. "You didn't say anything at my apartment."

"I would have stuttered."

She laughed with the playful response, forgetting about the men.

Sliding his arm behind her, he caught her unprepared as he moved smoothly to face her, pulling her close. She put one hand on his muscular arm and tipped her head up to look at him. Heat smoldered in his eyes and melted into her. She felt control slipping away and almost let go. Almost.

"What happened to One and Two?" She had to know.

The heat of his eyes cooled and a few seconds later he figured out what she was asking. He moved back from her and she lowered her hand. "I asked them both to marry me. First one said yes and six months after we were married a friend of mine told me he saw her with another man. Second one I asked to marry me just said no."

His quick rundown brushed over the top of two serious relationships, but they had to be the reason he hadn't asked Three to marry him. The one who'd mattered.

"Stop distracting me." He took a drink from his glass.

"I'm distracting you?" She sipped her champagne.

"Yes." The heat began returning to his eyes.

"From what?"

He put his drink on a cocktail table covered in white linen.

"From this." Pulling her close again, he inched his head down to hers. The warmth of his breath smelled sweet and alluring, and she almost dropped her glass.

"Mason?" Was he doing this on purpose or did he feel the trigger-fast eruption of desire like she did?

"Go with it."

When he pressed a kiss to her mouth, she wanted to put both hands on him but still held her glass. She had to settle for parting her lips to invite him in for more. He took it and kissed her harder for a second, but then backed off. Looking down at her, she thought she saw confusion before he looked over her head, up at the top of the stairs.

Go with it.

Chloe tensed.

She looked over her shoulder toward the second level. The man who'd stood there was descending the stairs. She watched with Mason as he approached them.

"Michael." He was a fortyish man whose aging face didn't match his fit shape. He shook Mason's hand.

"Donovan." Mason let the man's hand go and turned to Chloe. "This is Chloe. She and I met a month ago at the grocery store where she works."

"Ah, yes. Axel told me about her." He assessed her like a horse at an auction and then faced Mason. "I'm beginning to see why your trip to Florida was delayed."

Mason turned his grin to Chloe, who wanted to slap him at this point. He'd faked that kiss and she'd melted all over him!

"I only wonder why you'd take a woman you only just met home to meet your family."

"Chloe doesn't have any family here."

Donovan considered that for a few seconds and then nodded. "You know about Frankie?"

Mason's grin vanished. "Axel told me. I can't believe it."

"Everyone knows you and Frankie were friends. You must be upset."

"I never suspected he was anything other than what he seemed."

"Yes. It appears he had us all fooled." Donovan turned to Chloe. "Would you excuse us for a few moments?"

Her heart rushed into a frantic rhythm. Why? She looked at Mason.

"I'll be right back," he said to her, slipping his arm from around her.

Without waiting for her approval, Donovan led Mason up the stairs. She watched until they disappeared down a hallway.

A tall, thin man in a suit and holding a tray of champagne paused in front of her. She drank the rest of her glass, put it on the tray and took another.

"Thank you."

He gave her a slight bow and then went on his way.

She searched the crowd for the man Mason had encountered in the parking lot at Lawrence Tucker's. Axel. He wasn't there so she wondered if he was with Mason and Donovan. What were they going to do? Did they know Mason was an agent?

She glanced back at the front door. She'd stay close just in case.

Scanning the crowd again, she noticed several women wandering the room in short dresses. One of them talked to a man near a fireplace. He looked at her in a way that made Chloe's skin crawl. Another woman led a man up the stairs. Were these women here professionally? There weren't many couples in attendance. A few older women with men the same age.

She checked her watch. Any time now the raid would begin. Mason's boss had called him back and they'd discussed the logistics.

"Are you working tonight?"

Chloe turned her head to see a bald man with pitted skin standing beside her. She rolled her eyes at him and walked away, which was less than she wanted to do. Slugging him would have been more satisfying. Didn't these men know that most of the women didn't want to be here? She couldn't wait for the FBI to arrive.

Looking up toward the stairs, she spotted Mason descending them. Relieved, she reached the base of them just as he stepped off the last one. He guided her deeper into the crowd.

"Everything okay?" she asked.

"They're a little nervous, that's all."

She let the vague reply go. "I was propositioned while you were gone."

"I'd proposition you, too." He looked down at her dress.

She sent him a warning glance and he chuckled. Was he acting again or was his attraction real?

"I never wear dresses." The only reason she had this one was because of her ex-boyfriend. She'd worn it for him.

"You should wear them more often."

Maybe if she had a real reason to wear them.

The front doors banged open. "FBI! FBI! FBI! Don't move!"

Men in black Kevlar vests swarmed the room like invading bugs. Armed with pistols and automatic rifles, they came from everywhere. A few must have entered through the back of the house.

"Arms in the air!"

Chloe put her glass down and then lifted her arms with Mason. She glanced up the stairs as more agents ran up them. Donovan stood at the top, looking down at her and Mason as he was forced against the banister and handcuffed.

She looked for Axel but didn't see him. Agents checked identification and allowed some of the guests to leave through the front door.

One of the agents approached her and Mason.

"IDs," he said.

Mason pulled out his wallet and showed the man his badge. Chloe reached into her purse and opened her wallet. But the man waved it away.

"Agent Jaffee," he said, patting Mason on his shoulder. "Nice work, man."

"Not for Tanner."

"Yeah, I heard. But we got 'em." The agent looked around. "We got 'em."

Another man approached, this one dressed in slacks and a shirt under his bulletproof vest. He had short-cropped graying hair and hazel eyes.

"Reid," Mason said and the two shook hands.

"Good work, Jaffee. You've earned yourself a long vacation. Take as much time as you need."

"Thanks."

Reid looked at Chloe. "Is this the woman you told me about?"

"Yes. Chloe Bradford, Reid Richardson, the SAC."

"Special Agent in Charge," Reid said, taking her hand. "A pleasure, miss."

"Likewise."

"Thank you for cooperating with us. You've helped to free a lot of women tonight."

"No need to thank me." She was going to Montana to start a new life. Never mind an ache was beginning to expand because of Mason.

Two agents jerked Donovan toward the stairs, forcing him to step down them. All the while, he watched Mason talking to Reid.

"When are you going to Montana?" Reid asked.

"Tomorrow morning," Mason answered. "We have an early flight."

"We?" He looked from him to Chloe.

Mason seemed to realize his slip and glanced awkwardly at her. "I'm taking Chloe with me."

A flutter tumbled inside her when he said it. Was she really doing this? Going with Mason to his hometown in Montana?

"Really." Reid smiled at the two of them. "That's wonderful."

"It's not what you think," Mason quickly amended.

"He's taking me to Montana in exchange for helping him," Chloe wished she didn't feel so disappointed. "We had a deal."

Reid took a few seconds to process that. "I see." He didn't. Chloe could tell he was perplexed. "Well, it might be good for both of you to keep a low profile anyway, until we locate Axel."

"I agree," Mason said.

She wondered where the gravity of his tone came from. Was it an all-business wall of defense or was he more concerned about Axel on the loose than she thought?

Chapter 3

Mason kept looking at the rearview mirror as he drove them to the hotel where they'd check in for the night. Chloe's apartment was empty and she'd turned in a notice to her landlord. That had made leaving more real. This was it. She was leaving Chicago. Moving to Montana. It was exhilarating! And it helped take her mind off Mason.

His muttered curse broke her from thought. She looked over at him. His eyes kept going back and forth between the road and the rearview mirror. He turned a corner and checked the mirror again.

Chloe looked behind them. There were several cars on the road so she couldn't tell which one followed. When he turned another corner and a white SUV did the same, then she knew. What now?

Mason took another street. The SUV followed. When

he made yet another change in direction, the SUV kept going. The driver must know he'd been made.

"Do you think they know where we're staying?"

"No. We weren't followed to the hotel."

His certainty impressed her. He must have known to check for a tail. He probably did it out of habit or training.

Once they arrived at the hotel, Mason parked. Chloe climbed out of the rental and walked with him inside, not missing how he scanned the street first. After a short ride in the elevator, they reached their room. Mason took the card key from her and drew his gun before entering.

"Wait here," he said.

She held the door open until he finished doing a quick search.

"All clear, Agent Jaffee?" she teased, even though she actually appreciated his precaution. She was just at odds with his distant attitude.

He dropped his jacket onto one of the beds without acknowledging her. Maybe he was at odds with her, too, with being alone with her now that his job was finished.

"Let's order room service." They hadn't eaten dinner and her stomach was growling like mad. She didn't want to think about being alone with him.

"Good idea." Mason went to pick up the menu and she moved beside him to view it, too.

"The maple-glazed salmon with asparagus looks good. Two of those?" he asked.

"One. I'll have the macaroni and cheese."

"That's only on the kid's menu."

"Then get me two orders."

He lowered the menu. "I can afford something better. The Bureau will reimburse me."

"What's better than mac 'n' cheese?"

An incredulous lift to his brow followed. "Anything else on the menu."

Were they really arguing about food? "I want macaroni and cheese."

"Don't you eat vegetables?"

"If they're fried in something."

He just stared at her.

"Mac 'n' cheese, nothing else."

Shaking his head, he picked up the phone.

Maybe she'd only imagined her attraction to him. Did they have anything in common? He'd gone to college, had a flashy job and parents who lived on a ranch in Montana. And he liked fancy food. Dinner at home would be a mess.

Going into the bathroom, she washed her face and changed into pajamas. When she emerged, she sat cross-legged on one of the queen beds and began flipping through channels on the television.

Mason went into the bathroom and emerged bare-chested and in jeans. Chloe couldn't stop herself from ogling. He didn't seem to notice her reaction. Of course not. He thought she'd played along with him when he'd kissed her.

A knock on the door took him there and he let the attendant in. After the room door swung closed behind the man, Mason handed her the plate of mac 'n' cheese with a cynical frown. She took it and put it on her lap. He sat at the table and began to eat, glancing back at her.

"How's your macaroni and cheese?"

"Good." Cheesy.

"Do you eat meat?"

"Chicken fingers and cheeseburgers."

"No fish?"

"I like fish and chips."

He shook his head. "Steak?"

She smiled. "With sauce and fries."

He chuckled. "You should weigh a lot more than you do."

"It's all about portion control." And she couldn't afford big ones.

Finishing his meal, he took her plate and put the dishes on a tray outside the room. Then he went to the other bed and stretched out on it, leaning against pillows propped against the headboard, his stomach muscles bunching and keeping her gaze there.

"I think you should stay with me when we get to Montana."

She lifted her eyes to his profile. He hadn't turned to look at her when he spoke. And then it dawned on her that he wanted her to stay with him because of Axel. For a second she thought he meant because he liked her. "All I require is getting to Montana."

Mason rolled his head on his pillow. "Axel hasn't been located yet."

"I'm not afraid of him." How many men like that had she dealt with living in Chicago? Except, none of them had guns...

"Then humor me. I need you to stay with me until he's captured. Of all the men in that organization, Axel has the most reason to come after me."

"I don't want to stay with you any longer than I have to." More bite came out in her tone than she would have liked. She didn't understand her affront. Whatever happened to her heartache over her ex-boyfriend? Had one kiss obliterated him?

Now Mason swung his feet over the side of the bed and sat up. "Chloe…"

She picked up the remote again and flipped more channels, mad that he'd affected her that way.

"Chloe?"

Relenting, she dropped the remote and turned to look at him.

"Stay with me," he said.

Again, she was struck with the tantalization that he meant something other than he actually did. And then she recognized his worry. Did he think Axel would come after them? He'd said Axel had the most reason to do so.

"All right. I'll stay with you. But only until I get settled. Find a place to live. Start looking for a job."

"That's fine, as long as Axel is apprehended."

He was doing his job. Just like kissing her had been part of his job. "I understand. I can take care of myself, but I'll stay with you if it makes you feel better." She'd never admit to him that she agreed it was wise to be careful.

"I'm sure you can." He reclined on the bed again, sounding exhausted.

She tried to pay attention to another rendition of *A Christmas Carol*. But her awareness of him stopped her.

"What if Axel isn't caught by Christmas Day?" That was the day after tomorrow. "I don't want to intrude on your family."

"You won't intrude. My mother will hardly let you spend Christmas alone."

She glanced over at him. He'd closed his eyes with his hands behind his head. She let her gaze go over his bare chest.

"You'll like her," he said. "My dad, too."

She saw that his eyes were still closed.

"They know you worked with me on the investigation and why you're coming with me. You won't have to pretend you're my girlfriend."

"Good. Then you won't have to kiss me again."

His eyes opened and he rolled his head on the pillow again to see her.

She turned back to the TV. Why should it matter that he wasn't thinking of her with that kind of interest? He was just going to make sure she was all right and then she'd be on her own again. That would be the end of them. Whatever that was.

After suffering hours of traveling with Mason, landing in Great Falls and then renting a black GMC Yukon, Chloe's apprehension grew. Mason hadn't said much the entire trip. He seemed as unhappy as she was over having to stay close. The why of it had her in turmoil. What if he hadn't faked that kiss? Sure, it helped his cover, but had he felt the same as her? At the time it sure seemed that way. But he worked undercover. He role-played all the time.

They'd been following a snow-covered dirt road for several miles now. The endless beauty that passed her window captivated her every once in a while, offering a welcome reprieve from her thoughts. When Mason turned onto another road, she looked for a house but didn't see one. It was a few more miles before they rounded a curve and an old colonial-style house came into view.

Pure enchantment. It was big and white with black shutters and a wraparound porch with pillars in the front. There was a swing and a stone fountain that she was sure was absolutely beautiful in the summer.

"Oh," she breathed. "Is that...?"

"No. The log house up ahead is."

Looking forward she saw a sprawling log home with green metal roofing that screamed money.

"*That's* where your parents live?"

"Yes."

"Wow." That's all she could say. When he'd said his mother inherited a ranch she pictured a small farm-house. Smaller than this, anyway.

"My mom inherited the ranch. My great grandfather started up a bakery chain that took off...Schrader's?" He glanced at her and she nodded. She recognized the name. "It wasn't as big when he ran it. The corporation that bought it expanded quite a bit."

But he'd obviously done well in the sale.

"He bought this land and built the house when he sold the company and retired. My grandfather made a working ranch out of it. People rent the cabins he built."

"And your parents run the ranch now?"

"Yeah. That other one is the original house. I'll have to show you it some time. It's basically a guesthouse now. They built this log home three years ago."

"It's beautiful." Being around this kind of money was as foreign to her as a trip to Mongolia.

He stopped the Yukon in front of the log home. Warm light illuminated most of the windows in the front, the biggest beneath a huge triangular gable, where a giant Christmas tree twinkled cheerfully through the glass. Getting out of the SUV with him, she saw how he looked around before going to the front door to open the heavy wood door with a pretty wreath hanging on it. She wondered if the security measure was out of habit or if he was looking for Axel. That idea disconcerted her a little. It was so isolated here.

A horse whinnied. There must be a stable behind the house. Other than that, it was silent. No sounds of the city. Only absolute stillness beneath a partially cloudy sky.

Stepping inside behind Mason, her immediate impression was color and grandeur. A hall led off the living room beside a built-in entertainment center and an enormous television. The Christmas tree she saw from outside flirted with the beams overhead and inspired a new idea for a card. Opposite the entry, huge granite rocks rose from the fireplace to the exposed ceiling, nestled in the log wall.

"Mason? Is that you?" a female voice called.

"Hi, Mom."

"Karl! Mason's home!"

As Chloe moved farther into the room, she could see the kitchen around the gigantic tree and a stairway leading to a landing with two doors and a hallway. A woman with short, dark hair that was still shiny with health appeared from the kitchen, trotting toward them with a big smile. She was as tall as Chloe and a little thick around the middle, but not in a way that hindered her movement. She threw her arms around Mason and he hugged her back with a deep chuckle.

Then an older version of Mason emerged from a hallway to the left. His hair was still thick for his age and his green eyes smiled behind black-rimmed glasses. He was tall and lean, and Chloe thought in his younger years that he might have been a lot more muscular.

Mason's mom released him and his dad embraced him briefly. "It's been so long."

"Over a year," Mason said.

"How long before you're sent for another case?" his mother asked, her joy in seeing him deflating a bit. Each time he went undercover, the times he could see or talk to his family had to be limited. If Chloe had a family, she'd spend as much time as she could with them.

"I don't know. I'm taking a few weeks off."

Mason's vibrant mother turned her attention to Chloe, looking her up and down with a smile. "You didn't say she was pretty."

Taken off-guard, Chloe glanced uncertainly at Mason.

"Mom," he protested. "This is Chloe Bradford. My mother, Beverly." He turned to Karl. "My dad, Karl."

"Everyone calls me Bevy." She shook Chloe's hand firmly, letting go to let Karl shake it next, his much less vigorous.

"It's nice to meet you both." Bevy was the antithesis of her husband. Social energy beamed from her and Karl seemed like the quiet type. Chloe held back a grin.

"Thank you for helping my son," Bevy said. "Mason told me about how you had to pose as his girlfriend."

Chloe didn't miss Mason's fidgeting. He wanted to get these introductions over with. "We helped each other."

"Well, no matter what brought you together, we're so glad to have you for Christmas."

"I'm happy to be here." More than she should be, spending Christmas with a family…Mason's family.

"Where is everybody?" Mason asked.

"Your brother will be back in a while. He took the kids shopping in Great Falls," Karl said. Other than the subtle joy over seeing Mason when he first walked into the room, his expression remained stoic and unreadable.

"What about CC?"

His mother scoffed with a wave of her hand. "She said she'd be here last night but she had more drama to deal with before leaving L.A."

"What now?"

"Her husband is having an affair. He's spending Christmas with his lover. CC's a wreck."

It must be contagious. Everyone Chloe ran into lately had been with someone who left them for someone else.

"We'll fix her up when she gets here," Mason said.

Bevy kissed her son's cheek and patted the other one. "That's my son." Then she moved back. "You two can take two of the rooms upstairs. Go get your luggage, Mason. I'll take Chloe into the kitchen so we can get acquainted."

"I'll help you," Mason's father said, heading for the door.

Mason followed, casting a glance back at his mother and Chloe as though not sure he liked the idea of them getting acquainted. Chloe wasn't sure she did, either. Spending Christmas with his family was one thing, but getting too attached was quite another.

Bevy waved her toward the kitchen. "Come on. I'm getting ready for tonight."

She followed her into the kitchen, where the smell of Swedish meatballs grew stronger. "Do you celebrate on Christmas Eve?"

"The big event is tomorrow. I'm throwing together some appetizers for tonight." Bevy resumed rolling tortillas into spinach and cream cheese pinwheels.

"Mason said he met you at a grocery store."

"In the parking lot."

"I know he did what he had to at the time, running into one of those men he was investigating the way he did, but I have to tell you. I always hoped he would meet a nice girl that way. Without planning it. Spur of the moment. Out of the blue. When he least expects it."

Chloe began to pick up on some romanticized undercurrents. Did his mother think Mason had brought her here as his new girlfriend? Meeting him definitely hadn't been planned, but for him it was all business.

Just then, Mason and his dad came through the door along with the sound of many more voices. Boisterous voices. After everyone removed their winter coats, two blond-haired girls around six and eight roared with excitement and ran down the hall. An older, wiry blond-haired boy was slower and looked bored as he went to plop down in front of the television. Mason smiled as he talked to a man perhaps five to ten years older than him. His brother, the homicide detective. He was shorter than Mason and had light brown hair. A slender blond-haired woman in a soft green sweater followed beside Mason's father, talking rapidly with a big, toothy smile. She waved into the kitchen.

Then the four of them climbed the stairs, carrying shopping bags and luggage, loud chatter fading as they turned down the hall.

"It's not often Mason brings a girl home," Bevy commented.

Chloe turned back to her, again picking up on the leading insinuation. "He thought it was best."

Bevy eyed her briefly, appearing unconvinced that was the only reason. Her dark hair was a stylish bob around her aging face and her gray eyes were keen with intelligence.

Catching sight of Mason stepping down the stairs ahead of his father and brother, she found herself unable to stop looking at him. He moved smooth and strong, all man coming toward her. He noticed her and their gazes held. When he reached the bottom, he gave her a subtle grin before turning to go into the living room.

The blonde came jogging down the stairs, still in jeans and the green sweater. Not as tall as Chloe, she had big breasts and hips that were probably hard to keep trim. She entered the kitchen.

"Deirdra, this is Chloe Bradford, Mason's friend."

The way Bevy said *friend* clearly indicated she didn't believe for a minute they were just friends.

"It's about time Mason brought someone home," Deirdra said, obviously having drawn the same conclusion as Bevy. She sat on the stool next to Chloe, blue eyes dancing, shoulder-length blond hair thick and shining.

"Any luck shopping?" Bevy asked.

"Yes. We found what you were looking for." Just as Chloe began to wonder what that was, she continued, "Teddy bought four new movies." She smiled over at Chloe. "Why is it that we always end up buying more than we plan at Christmastime?"

Chloe didn't know what that was like. She just smiled amicably and kept quiet.

The front door opened again and Chloe noticed it was dark outside. A woman appeared around the Christmas tree, rolling a suitcase to a stop and draping her fur-hooded jacket over the top as Mason reached her. After hugging him and talking a bit, she embraced her dad and other brother. In tight stretch jeans with colorful butterflies running down one thigh and a wild sparkly printed long-sleeved shirt, she had a vibrancy that matched her mother's. Her hair had a blond streak in the dark strands and her eye makeup was heavy around green eyes that were the same color as Mason's. She ruffled the boy's blond head before heading toward the kitchen.

"CC." Bevy moved around the kitchen island to hug her. "Are you okay?"

"I'm great. My husband is bonking a twelve-year-old."

"You're only twenty-seven, Cees. She can't be that much younger than you."

"I knew he was too in love with himself. I should have never married the weasel."

"I won't say I told you so."

"Thanks, Mom." CC noticed Chloe then. "One of the neighbors come over for Christmas again?"

"No, this is Mason's girlfriend," Deirdra said.

Breathing an entertained laugh, Bevy went to remove some shrimp from the refrigerator.

"I'm not his—"

"Chloe Bradford, meet Mason's younger sister, CC Jaffee," Dierdra cut her off.

"It's not Jaffee anymore."

"It will be again soon."

CC smirked at the unwanted truth and then went to the refrigerator. "Mason didn't say anything to me about a girlfriend." She closed the refrigerator door, holding a beer.

"We're just friends," Chloe insisted.

"She posed as Mason's girlfriend to help him protect his cover," Bevy said, arranging the shrimp in a pretty bowl. "But they met at a grocery store before that."

CC used a bottle opener to remove the cap and then came to sit on the other side of Chloe. "He still in that dumpy part of Chicago?"

"That's where Mason met Chloe," Bevy informed the blunt-speaking woman. "She lives there."

"Oh." CC looked apologetically at Chloe. "Sorry."

Mason's rich laughter made her look into the living room. The sight of his still-smiling face stole her concentration. Catching her watching, his smile faded and his eyes took on a telling smolder.

Forcing her attention back to CC after a notable delay, she said, "Don't be. It *is* a dumpy part of Chicago. That's why I'm moving here."

After following Chloe's gaze, Deirdra lifted her brow speculatively.

"You're moving here?" CC asked.

"Yes. But not because…not because…" Why couldn't she say not because of Mason? She wasn't moving here for him. But these women thought…

"Why did he bring you home with him?" CC asked.

"The FBI is still looking for one of the men Mason was investigating. It's a precautionary measure," Bevy said. "He didn't want to leave her in Chicago."

It was more than precautionary. And it had nothing to do with his interest in her. He wasn't interested. Was he? She glanced over at him again but he was busy talking to his dad.

No. He was worried Axel would find them here. That was why she'd agree to stay with him. She looked out the dining room window, darkness peering in between the swooping curtains. She'd seen how he had scanned their surroundings on the way here. His family thought the danger was left behind in Chicago, but Mason was afraid of bringing danger to their door.

"I think that's what he'd like us all to believe," Deirdra said, reeling her back into the conversation. "I bet he likes her."

"Oh, I doubt—"

"I saw the way you look at each other," Deirdra teased. "It's obvious."

Was it? Mason didn't seem open to letting another woman into his heart.

CC laughed lightheartedly. "This is going to be a great Christmas. Exactly what I need."

"Really, I don't think—"

"You're different than the other three he brought here," Deirdra interrupted again.

Bevy was smiling in that way again. "She does seem different."

Chloe checked each woman's face and settled on Bevy, relenting to curiosity. "How so?"

"Not as fancy," CC said. "They all made more money than him."

The woman didn't know when she was insulting. Chloe found it refreshing, though.

"CC, stop," Bevy said.

"What?" her daughter queried.

"It's okay," Chloe said. "I won't always live in the slums."

CC's eyes went round with appall. "Oh my gosh. I'm so sorry. I totally didn't mean it that way. It's just that Mason...well, he always falls for such stuffy women. I mean, they're pretty and all, but they don't have personalities. He can't pick them very well."

"That's the problem," Bevy said, "*They* chase *him* down, he doesn't get a chance to pick them himself. Chloe he met in a grocery store parking lot and dating wasn't even on his mind."

"That's true," CC agreed, nodding. "The first one worked with him and she was all over him."

"She was an FBI agent?" Chloe asked, too curious for her own good.

"No, she was some kind of director or something."

"She was a bitch," Deirdra said. "When she discovered she couldn't ball-break him, she left him for someone else."

"The second one was a college professor," CC went on.

Deirdra rolled her eyes. "Yeah, physics of all things. Why was he interested in a woman like that? And how did he meet her? She was weird. Quiet and self-conscious, like she felt she had to bring herself down an intellectual level just so she could be around us."

"No wonder that didn't last," Bevy said.

"She picked him up at a trendy bar," CC said, tucking her blond-streaked hair behind her ear. "I think she was looking for a stay-at-home dad. So when he told her he wouldn't change jobs..."

"And then he met that engineer," Bevy said.

The third one. The one Chloe could tell had hurt him the most. The one he'd said he should have married.

"She was actually nice. I liked her," CC said.

"Yeah, me too," Deirdra said. "She was normal."

Chloe didn't like the sound of this, especially since it made her feel the same way her boyfriend had when he broke up with her. Second-best. Not his number one choice.

"Talking about me?"

With a sparkle of awareness, Chloe turned along with the other women to see Mason approaching, sexy in jeans and a blue knit sweater. She wished she didn't find him so attractive, and all the leading inflections from the female population of his family were getting to her. He must have heard a good portion, if not all of the conversation and she wondered if that's what had drawn him in here. He probably wanted to put a stop to it.

"We were just asking Chloe why you brought her here," CC said, not missing a beat.

He stopped behind Chloe and Deirdra at the island. "I already told Mom. I have to be sure the investigation is officially closed. She was seen with me. I don't want anything to happen to her."

There was nothing personal about his answer, but she noticed a flicker of something in his eyes that hinted to the possibility of more. Was it a struggle to keep this professional? Was he struggling like her?

"Chicago is a long way from here," CC said.

Mason blinked and the possibility vanished. "Right, and that's why I brought her here."

That was true. Protecting her had been his initial motivation, but something else was brewing between them, something neither of them was ready for. Checking the darkened window, he quickly covered any sign of concern, but not before his mother noticed.

Bevy searched her son's face but he didn't satisfy her curiosity.

"Well." Bevy dried her hands on a towel. "It's good you brought her here. It doesn't matter why. No one should be alone on Christmas."

"I'm not alone. I have a lot of friends in Chicago."

Crap. Why had she said that? She could see each and every one of them looking at her curiously. They all wondered the same thing. Why had she uprooted her life to come here? If she wasn't alone in Chicago, she'd most certainly be alone here.

"What matters is you're here," Bevy said with a clever and delighted smile in her eyes. "You just…

popped right into Mason's life. Anything else will resolve itself."

"Mom…" Mason warned.

"You know what they say about love," Deirdra said.

"It happens when you least expect it," CC supplied the answer with a brief laugh.

Chloe looked back at Mason and speculation passed between them. What if something did start between them? A fleeting shimmer of heat entered into the exchange, quickly followed by wariness.

Mason cleared his throat and stepped back.

Chloe picked up a pinwheel and pretended nothing had happened. As alluring as finding love and a family like this one was, along with the possibility of truly belonging to it, she could not risk the repercussions. Not now. Not yet.

Chapter 4

After breakfast on Christmas morning, Chloe descended the stairs. Christmas music played and she could hear the snap crackle of a fire. The door at the bottom of the stairs was open. There was a rec room in the basement and she could hear the kids down there. Voices and clattering dishes confirmed at least some of the family was in the kitchen, the hangout for the holidays. She was looking forward to today.

Last night she'd eaten appetizers with Mason's family and watched two of the movies Teddy had picked up while the kids kept asking if they could open presents. Bevy had made fried mushrooms and shrimp scampi on French bread that was dripping with butter. Chloe had been in heaven with the fried mushrooms and bread. She'd been in even greater heaven with Mason sitting across the room from her. Every once in a while she caught him watching her, and each look sizzled more than the last. She wondered if hearing his mother and sisters talking about how different she was than his previous girlfriends had gotten to him.

She'd tried to dismiss the significance by striking up a conversation with CC. She learned she was a hairdresser and that her mother thought she'd move on to something else. Something better. They'd bonded and if CC didn't live in L.A., Chloe would want to keep her for a friend.

Reaching the bottom of the stairs, she collided with none other than Mason on her way into the kitchen. Her hands came against his dark green heavy cotton shirt and she felt his on her hip bones. Eyes she hadn't been so close to since they'd kissed flared with the same affliction that had been in them last night. He was freshly shaven and smelled sweet and spicy.

"I was just coming to get you," he murmured.

"Here I am." An awkward response, but hopefully it hid the heat that consumed her being this close to him.

He dropped his hands and stepped back. "Everyone's ready for the sleigh ride."

A sleigh ride? Chloe had only painted them.

"It's a family tradition," he explained with a note of dread. "Every year on Christmas morning, we go for a sleigh ride."

Could this Christmas be any more enchanting? Chloe decided not to stop herself from enjoying every second. She'd have a fond memory. It might come with bittersweet regret later, but what harm would it bring? It didn't have to be any different than those spent with her friends' families. She was with a family on Christmas. So what if it was Mason's?

Just then, Bevy emerged from the kitchen and saw them. With a knowing smile, she handed Chloe a

Thermos of hot cocoa and then a blanket to Mason. "Share that with her."

He grumbled something and started for the coat rack. Chloe followed. Outside, a sleigh and four Clydesdales waited in the snow. The horses were adorned with brass bells and the sleigh was garnished with pine branches and big red boughs.

"Oh," she couldn't help exclaiming.

Mason lifted her up to the step of the sleigh. She climbed in, tingling from where he'd touched her. He climbed in after her. Deirdra and her family were already sitting on the two middle seats.

Chloe sat in the back, feeling like a kid again. The seat was smaller back here and only fit two, like the front seat. The two middle seats were wider with the shape of the sleigh.

Mason sat next to her and wrapped the blanket around them both. She snuggled close to him and played down the significance of his arm around her. His parents climbed up into the driver's seat and CC sat next to her little nieces. The older boy sat between his parents.

Karl urged the Clydesdales into a walk and the sleigh jerked into motion. Chloe would not be able to remove the smile from her face until the ride was over. She wanted to see everything, not miss a thing. Mason noticed and she saw his warming look.

The sleigh passed the old colonial house Mason's grandfather had built. Chloe vowed she'd design a Christmas card that would capture all of its cozy grandeur. She craned her neck to see it as they passed, and when she turned forward again, saw that Mason had taken notice of her appreciation.

He told her he'd take her there, but he hadn't yet.

They followed the snow-covered driveway until they reached the road she and Mason had driven in on. The overcast sky confirmed what she'd heard on the news this morning. Another storm was moving in.

The Clydesdales sped up into a trot, sleigh bells ringing. This would be a Christmas she'd never forget!

A truck passed them from the opposite direction and Karl and Bevy waved. They came upon a convenience store and gas station that also offered a few cabin rentals. Christmas lights glimmered. A man gathered wood in a wheelbarrow and paused to wave with a smile.

They all waved back.

Chloe tucked her hand under the blanket. It landed on Mason's thigh. She sensed him turn her way. Instead of moving her hand, she gave in to what her heart called for her to do and leaned her head on his shoulder. He went still for a second, but then she felt his hand cover hers and hold it. Chloe closed her eyes and concealed a contented sigh. This shouldn't feel as good as it did.

"Are you warm?"

Mason's deep voice was full of intimacy.

"Yes." Her sultry reply fueled the stirring desire between them.

She could kiss him right now. She wanted to. Badly enough to throw caution aside. She tipped her head up just a little, just enough.

What seemed like minutes passed before he touched her mouth with his. She felt flushed and out of breath. Fireworks burst and spread. Her heart raced.

Mason looked down at her as they both settled back to Earth, then turned toward the front of the sleigh, making Chloe do the same. No one had noticed.

Another vehicle approached, this one a sedan, driving slow over the snow-packed road. Karl and Bevy waved again, but the driver didn't wave back. As the sedan passed, Chloe saw him. *Was that Axel?*

Startled, she looked up at Mason.

"Don't look back," he said. "He didn't see us."

Oh God. It was him. Her heart raced anew, but as a result of something far less pleasant.

"How did he find us?"

"He must have figured out my name. My parents don't hide their address."

"Your partner must have told them. The other agent?" Even though Axel had said he hadn't talked before they'd killed him, what if he had? Now she understood why Mason had been so worried Axel would follow them.

"Donovan said he was waiting for Axel when he brought me to the room to question me. He said the party would get started then."

Meaning, the party with Mason and her?

"One of the questions he asked me is what I thought the feds had on them. I told him they couldn't have anything. I doubt he suspected there'd be a raid as soon as that night, but I bet he knew about New Year's Eve."

Tanner had told them? "Why wait for Axel, then? If he knew you were an agent…"

"No one in that organization wanted me dead more than Axel."

So Donovan agreed to wait? She watched the passing landscape, but the enchantment was gone. "It's personal to him?"

"He hated that Donovan befriended me, favored me in some cases. Agreed with my ideas more than his. That always sent him over the edge. If it hadn't been for Donovan and his henchmen, Axel would have tried to kill me a long time ago."

"And now that Donovan is out of the way…"

"Along with everyone else…"

There was nothing stopping him from killing Mason now. He was here in Woodland, Montana to do just that. He'd found them. Chloe shivered.

"What if he's on the way to the house?"

Mason adjusted his arm around her. "I doubt he'll try anything today. He'll probably find a warm place to stay for the night. It's Christmas. Besides that, my entire family is here. My brother's a homicide detective. Between the two of us, we could take care of him."

She hoped so. She wasn't an easy target for bad men, but Axel was worse than any she'd encountered. He had a gun. Glancing behind them once more and not seeing Axel's car, she turned forward again.

"I won't let anything happen to you," Mason said. "Or my family."

Smiling, she leaned her head against his shoulder again. Knowing she had an FBI agent watching over her went a long way to ease her mind. Besides, she didn't want anything to ruin this wonderful day.

CC caught sight of them and elbowed her nephew under the blanket they shared. The boy pushed the blanket off him and gave it to her, not showing any interest in Chloe and Mason. A teenager alone in the middle of nowhere probably spelled boredom. That's when she saw him texting. Distracted, not bored. She hoped he didn't do that when he drove.

By noon, they arrived back at the turn for the Jaffees' ranch. Chloe noticed a sign she hadn't seen on the way here the first time. Snowy Meadow Lodge. Nice. What a dream she was having. She wished she'd never wake up.

"Hey, Dad," Mason called.

Karl turned along with everyone else except the two young girls.

"Stop here so we can shut the gate."

"Why?"

"Just do it."

His mother looked with concern at Karl, who slowed the Clydesdales to a stop. His quiet nature worked to keep the rest of them calm. Shrugging the blanket off his shoulders, Mason climbed off the sleigh and walked back to where the gate was chained open. His dad and brother joined him and Chloe could see them talking. Karl closed the gate without a fuss and locked it with the chain. There were steep ditches on both sides of the driveway and the snow was deep where it wasn't plowed. It would be difficult to get to the driveway in a vehicle. Axel had been driving a sedan. She looked for unfamiliar tracks in the snow. There were none. Just as Mason had predicted, Axel hadn't gone to the house. He'd only scoped out its location. Chloe tightened the blanket against another shiver.

"What's going on?" CC asked her mother.

"I don't know."

Karl climbed onto the front seat and Teddy and Mason took their seats. For the first time since Chloe had seen him, Teddy wore a detective's mask, grim and deep in thought as he put their blanket back around them. His wife had noticed, too.

"Why do you want the gate closed, Mason?" CC asked.

"Just a precaution."

Her head whipped around as she searched the surrounding landscape and road. "Do you think someone might come after you? That man you didn't arrest during your raid? Axel or whatever his name was? He got away. Do you think he'd come all the way here?"

Deirdra exchanged another worried look with her husband, who kissed her briefly before turning to Mason. "We'll be ready just in case."

"Oh, great. Just what we need. An armed Christmas." CC shook her head.

"Awesome," the teenager said.

Karl set the Clydesdales into motion.

The sky was grayer now, the clouds lower and a frigid breeze had picked up.

While Mason helped his dad and Teddy put away the horses, Chloe went inside with the others. She could smell the turkey cooking and wanted to savor the aroma. While the other three went into the kitchen, chattering away about the prospect of one of Mason's criminals coming after them, she went to the fireplace and added more wood.

"Do you think that man will come here? Are we all in danger?" Chloe heard Deirdra ask.

"And do you really think locking that stupid gate is going to keep anyone out?" CC added.

"Teddy wouldn't be concerned if he didn't think there was a reason," Deirdra said.

"Enough," Bevy demanded. "I need help making a green salad and scalloped potatoes. So come on, we could use the distraction."

"I'll make the salad," Deirdra said.

"CC, why don't you wash potatoes and peel them?"

Straightening from the fireplace, Chloe entered the kitchen last. "What can I do?"

"You can help me get the appetizers ready. They're in the fridge." Bevy open the oven and took the turkey out to check it.

Chloe found the leftovers from last night and began to put them on the counter. CC got the potatoes out and began washing them next to her while Bevy basted the turkey at the oven. Deirdra took over the kitchen island with the salad prep.

"What happened on Mason's assignment, Chloe?" CC asked quietly. "Why is Mason so worried?" Her dark mascara popped out her crystal clear green eyes, and her long-sleeved red shirt with its colorful beaded front matched her personality.

"I don't think he's that worried." Yet.

"Why did he want the gate closed, then?"

Chloe didn't know how to answer that.

"Were you two followed here?"

Again, she hesitated, remembering the SUV that had nearly followed them to the hotel.

CC dropped a wet potato onto the counter. "Oh, my God, you were!"

She faced the three women. "Not here. In Chicago. No one followed us to the airport and no one followed us here." She didn't say what Mason had told her, that his parents were easy to find, or that Tanner could have talked after having the information tortured out of him.

"Stop worrying, Cees," Teddy entered the kitchen ahead of Mason and Karl. "Nothing's going to happen tonight. And even if it does, do you think you're in the company of amateurs?"

CC resumed her work washing potatoes. "Don't be cocky, Teddy. You've seen more death than all of us in this room."

Chloe saw how Deirdra looked at her husband and felt empathy for her. CC had aired something that bothered the woman. Her husband was a homicide detective. That meant he was sometimes in the line of fire and when he wasn't, he must carry unimaginable horrors with him.

Seeing her look, Teddy went to his wife and rubbed her back, leaning down for a kiss. Deirdra smiled up at him, comforted.

First looking over at Mason, Karl went over to his wife and they exchanged words only the two of them could hear. Bevy nodded with a loving smile, his unruffled way clearly what soothed her.

Looking back at Mason, seeing his furrowed brow, she felt his angst. He hadn't wanted his family to know he'd considered the possibility that Axel would follow him here. Maybe he even thought he could handle it on his own and now he wasn't so sure. Axel had followed them here. Had he told his dad? Teddy? Probably, and the men would stop at nothing to protect their family.

Mason met her gaze and she offered him a supportive smile. Some of his tension eased and it amazed her that she was able to do that for him. He blinked and then something other than tension made its way into his green eyes. She wished she could go over to him now. The fact that she couldn't sobered her. Torn, she put all her attention into heating the leftovers and making them presentable on the kitchen island.

When she finished, Mason handed her a glass of wine. She took it and noticed he held a beer. She'd rather have that, but she didn't tell him.

"Chloe, will you take the cheese and crackers and that spinach dip out to the coffee table? We're going to open presents before dinner. That way, after we eat all this food the adults can take a nap while the kids play with their presents." She zeroed in on CC. "No more drama. It's Christmas. Nothing more exciting than overeating and tearing wrapping paper is going to happen for the rest of the night."

"Mom," CC complained.

"CC?"

Even Chloe would heed that look. Smiling, she put her wine down and lifted the plate of cheese and crackers.

"I'll help you." Mason put his beer down and carried the spinach dip.

She put the crackers down with his spinach.

"Have a seat, I'll get your wine."

Was it her imagination or was Mason being especially attentive toward her? For real. Unlike at the party, he hadn't pretended when he'd kissed her on the sleigh. She watched his jean-clad butt as he returned to the kitchen and didn't care if he noticed her checking the rest of him out when he returned.

He handed her the glass and sat right next to her. This was very different than last night. Chloe decided to chalk it up to Christmas cheer and ignore the little voice in her head that said, *beware of mistletoes.*

Chapter 5

Mason watched Chloe as his family opened presents. He could tell she enjoyed just being a part of it. He didn't want to love that about her. It humbled her, made her real. Honest. Even worse, he didn't think any other woman he'd fallen for would have appreciated everyone else getting presents while all they could do is watch.

His mom handed him the present he'd been waiting for. He shared a secretive look with her before she turned and went back to the tree to resume passing gifts out between opening her own.

Chloe looked over at him when he didn't move to open the present, her short, thick blond hair bobbing a little with the movement. He waited, savoring the moment.

"Aren't you going to open it?"

"Nope."

Perplexity sparkled in her pretty blue eyes, as if she were wondering if he was kidding. "Why not?"

"Because this is for you." He handed it to her, loving the O her lips formed in her surprise.

"For me?" Taking the present, she looked at his mom for confirmation.

"Mason told me what you needed."

Turning to him, she whispered, "Mason."

It was the sweetest sound he'd ever heard. It stirred his desire as much as kissing her had. He barely knew this woman and already he wanted to pursue her. Experience had taught him the folly of following his heart, but his heart made him want to take her to bed.

Chloe began to open the present, unaware that his entire family had stopped what they were doing to watch. Tearing the wrapping paper, she pulled out the portfolio case he'd asked his mother to find for him and Deirdra had picked up when she and Teddy had gone shopping.

She pushed the paper aside slowly, entranced by the realization of what it was. Unzipping it, she opened the case and saw its varied functions. She could put all her mock-ups in there, use it for safe storage or easily carry it for solicitation purposes.

Tears moistened her eyes as she turned to look at him. "This is the most thoughtful gift anyone has ever given me."

She meant it. He could see the truth in her eyes and hear it in her voice.

When she leaned over to him, he wasn't expecting her to kiss his face.

Her kind of appreciation was hard to ignore. "You're welcome."

She put her hand on the side of his face and turned

his head, kissing him on the mouth. He kissed her back without thinking. That ended up in a third kiss that was longer. He slid his hand behind her head and gave in to desire. By the time he drew away and could pry his eyes off her, it was too late for damage control. The room was a flutter of delighted snickers and whispers.

"Hey. I can't afford another trip until after my divorce, so you're going to have to wait to get married," CC said, and everyone laughed.

While Chloe's face colored, his mom passed out the rest of the presents. Mason struggled to pay attention. He still burned from kissing Chloe.

With the presents opened and the kids taking a break from playing after lengthy protests, Chloe followed Mason and the rest of his family into the dining area. Bevy had put a tablecloth on and set it with her china.

Chloe stopped with Mason under the archway, waiting for everyone to get settled while Karl and Bevy brought food to the table.

"Hey, look where you're standing," Deirdra said, pointing above Chloe's and Mason's heads.

Mistletoe.

The irony just about killed her. She saw Mason's hesitation and would have backed away, except CC was standing behind her and gave her a shove.

"Come on. We already know you two are kissing each other, what's the harm in kissing once more?"

Chloe wasn't sure she could take another kiss.

"In this house, whenever someone stands under the mistletoe, you have to honor tradition," Bevy said. Beside her, Karl eyed his wife as though not surprised she'd be the one to enforce such a rule.

"Kiss her."

"Kiss her."

"Kiss her…"

The chanting went on with a clamor.

Grinning, Mason slipped his arms around her, pulling her against him. She rested her hands on his chest, heart slamming.

"You better make it good, too," Bevy goaded.

Someone took a picture.

Mason leaned down, a smile in his eyes. Chloe was game for a quick one. His lips pressed to hers. The kisses before this one were the warm-up. Sweet tingles of pleasure spread across her skin, only to melt in her heart and turn into molten desire.

With catcalls from his family, she wrapped her arms around him and took him in for deeper exploration, too absorbed in Mason for the audience to matter. Endless seconds passed. She wanted them to go on forever.

Finally, Mason pulled back. His green eyes glowed with passion.

"That'll be one to remember," CC said, fanning herself.

"I'll send you the pictures, Mason," Deirdra said.

"Let's eat," Mason said, turning and heading for the table.

Awkwardly, Chloe followed, wondering if anyone other than her had picked up on his stiff withdrawal.

The lighthearted snickers and giggles lasted until after everyone sat down and Bevy said a prayer. Mason sat close to her, his right arm, brushing hers as he used his fork. Deirdra and CC got into a discussion about hairstyles. Karl and Teddy talked politics. Bevy asked her teenaged grandson to stop texting at the table.

Chloe loved every nuance. Dare she ever hope to have this again? Even with her ex-boyfriend it hadn't been this poignant. Something about this family... Mason...rang true.

Glancing over at him, she stopped the thought. Would his past experiences ruin any chance they had? She didn't think she had the strength to try. It was too soon after her last heartbreak. She wasn't prepared for another one, especially one she feared would hurt more than that.

Mason put his hand over hers and curled his fingers around her palm, holding her hand. A silent agreement passed between them, a stay of execution. For today they'd forget the heartaches that made them reluctant to trust again. Today was a day of hope. Maybe that was why thoughts of Axel had drifted so far from her conscience. How could she worry about him when this day was so perfect?

After helping to clear the table and get the kitchen under control, Chloe went into the living room, where the guys had a movie playing. Mason moved to the end of the sofa, leaning against a fluffy pillow. He patted the space between his legs. She was drawn by the look in his eyes. Sitting close, she leaned against his him.

The movie fell into the background. She was only aware of Mason. His hard chest against her back. His face beside hers when she rested it against his shoulder. The way his hands toyed with hers in gentle play. The warmth of his breath. When his defenses lowered and he let her in like this, it was almost more than she could take.

Deirdra, her husband and kids were the first to go to bed. Mason's parents were next. CC turned on another movie.

Not wanting the night to end, Chloe sat up and looked back at Mason. He seemed as indecisive as her.

Would tomorrow change what had transpired between them today? Would he withdraw behind a wall again? She didn't want to know.

"Good night, CC," Chloe said, standing.

"Night. Night, Mason."

Mason hadn't even gotten up yet. But now he answered and stood with Chloe. Her heart beat with unreasonable desire as he followed her up the stairs and down the hall. Her room was at the end.

She listened to him stop at his room. Stopping at hers, she stood in the doorway, wanting him to follow. Unreasonably. Neither of them moved.

Not sure about inviting him in, she left it up to him. After leaving the door open, she removed her clothes and climbed onto the bed, lying in the dark, tortured by anticipation.

She saw his silhouette in the doorway. Her heart rejoiced with needy beats. He closed the door and moved to the foot of the bed, standing there for a while. She could see his eyes through the shadows and he could probably see hers, just as on fire as his.

Pushing the covers off her, she let that be her answer. She wasn't wearing anything. He unbuttoned his jeans and shoved them off along with his underwear. Then he crawled onto the bed, on his hands and knees above her. He lowered himself to kiss her.

Their breathing resonated in the room. He put his knees between hers and she made room for him. He lowered onto her, still on his hands as he kissed her with more fervor. She ran her hands up his arms to his shoulders, his skin soft to her touch, but hard and sinewy underneath.

When he pulled his mouth from hers, she tipped her head back to bring her mouth closer to his, not wanting him to stop kissing her. Moving down to her breast, he took her nipple instead. She moaned her approval. His breath cooled and then warmed her skin as he moved from there to her stomach, progressing along her body until he found the place he'd endeavored to go. She dug her fingers into his hair. It wouldn't take much to send her over the edge.

"Come back here," she said.

He kissed his way back to her mouth, slow and tortuous. Reaching between their bodies, he guided himself to her warm wetness and pushed into her. The initial penetration robbed her of breath. He grunted his pleasure as he pushed back and forth. She loved the sound. The delicious friction of his steady thrusts sparked unbearable sensations that kept building until an orgasm crashed upon her.

He kissed her without stopping, sliding into her and pulling back over and over, going deeper now. Harder. He stimulated her still sensitive flesh. Looking up into his pleasure-filled eyes, finding it wholly erotic, another orgasm erupted. His guttural moan followed, his face a contortion of ecstasy.

Floating back down to normalcy, she curled next to him when he lay beside her, each of them catching their breath. So many thoughts assailed her. How would this change them? Would it change them at all? What if he had regrets? What if she woke up with regrets?

"Well, that's one way to get over being dumped," she quipped, needing levity.

He chuckled. "Glad to be of service."

Realizing she'd just given him an out, Chloe lay awake for a long time. She pretended to be asleep when she felt him get off the bed, listening to him pull on his jeans. With anguish tugging at her heart, she watched his silhouette leave the room, closing the door behind him without a sound.

The anguish mushroomed until it consumed her. She stared up at the ceiling, struggling not to fall apart. Why had he left before morning? Was he afraid of what his family would think? Or had he just run away? Yes, he was running. To him, she wasn't worth the risk of falling in love. She wasn't someone he wanted to have feelings for.

She should have never allowed the enchantment of Christmas to bring her guard down. She should have waited until she was sure of what Mason wanted out of this, out of them. It burned her to learn that was nothing. Nothing, of course, other than what they'd just done.

She was here for Christmas and that's all. She was going to start a new life, and that had nothing to do with Mason. He had a life of his own in Chicago—if that was where he actually lived. She didn't even know that much about him. She should have never allowed them to be intimate so soon.

"Stupid girl," she said.

But fool her once…

Chapter 6

Fortified with resolve, Chloe descended the stairs. Voices and dishes clanging in the kitchen filled her with regret. The day after Christmas, the family all still together, happy and content. She didn't belong. After Mason left her last night and she got over her anger, a calm sort of certainty took over. He'd made his decision. Now it was time for her to make hers.

She didn't care where she spent the night tonight as long as it wasn't here. All she needed was a way into town. While Axel could still be a threat, she'd lived alone in a rough neighborhood long enough to put that fear to rest. She needed to get away from Mason more than she was afraid of an encounter with an vengeful pimp.

Entering the kitchen, she saw Bevy first, busy as usual with preparing a meal. Chloe spotted Mason next, sitting at the table with his nephew and Deirdra. He saw her and froze for a second. The telltale sign stung so much that her resolve slipped.

"Good morning," Bevy greeted cheerily.

"Good morning." Chloe knew she sounded much less jovial.

Mason stood up and brought his plate to the sink as if she weren't even there. Bending to kiss his mom on the cheek, he said, "Thanks, Mom. I'll be out in the woodshed with Dad and Teddy."

Bevy glanced at Chloe and then back at her son in confusion. He moved away from her and approached Chloe, his mask of indifference ice-cold.

He was shutting her out, the wall he'd erected impenetrable. They'd shared a rare and gripping intimacy and he was going to pretend nothing happened. It had meant the world to her and he was throwing it away as if it belonged in the trash. He may as well throw it at her face. Slap her with it.

Rising anger only marginally eased the intense ache that expanded in her chest. She had no one to blame but herself for this. He hadn't forced her to sleep with him. She'd invited him.

"Chloe." The halfhearted greeting sounded forced. He didn't want to be anywhere near her.

"Mason," she echoed, fighting the magnitude of her inner turmoil. She may as well be one of his sister's friends he'd met for the first time.

Passing her, he left the kitchen, each step farther away mounting her emptiness. Bevy had stopped screwing the cap on a container of orange juice as she watched. She looked at Chloe when Mason disappeared.

"It smells incredible in here," Chloe said, refusing to allow Mason's handicap with women to bring her down.

He wasn't worth hurt feelings if he couldn't recognize a good thing when it landed right in front of him.

"Grab a plate," Bevy said.

Chloe did, but only for something to do while her emotions spun in circles. After spooning some cheesy eggs and ham onto a plate, she picked up one of the glasses of orange juice Bevy had poured and went to the table.

Bevy sat across from her with her own plate and juice. "Mason is awfully quiet this morning."

Chloe chewed some eggs and swallowed. Normally she would have loved all the cheese in them, but today they may as well be raw vegetables.

CC entered the kitchen. "What's wrong with Mason? I just saw him at the front door and teased him about Chloe and he just about bit my head off."

Chloe didn't look up from her plate.

CC sat beside her mother and Chloe felt them both watching her. Eating more eggs, she finally met their looks.

"Uh oh," CC said.

"Mason's got himself a problem, it would seem," Bevy added.

That's right, Mason had a problem. She didn't. "He does seem a little off this morning." She continued to eat, hoping that would be the end of it.

But both Bevy and CC had stopped eating. They each shared a glance and then resumed looking at Chloe.

"Is everything okay?" CC asked.

Did she really have to answer that? Seeing the concern on each of their faces, she put her fork down. "I'm really grateful for everything, but I need to leave today."

Silence. Bevy and CC exchanged another look.

"You slept with him, didn't you," CC observed.

"CC," Bevy admonished.

"It's written all over her face. And Mason flew into a fit when I teased him." She turned pointedly to her mother. "You saw them last night."

"Enough, CC. Chloe, whatever happened between you and Mason, it's all right. You can still stay here."

Chloe shook her head. "No. I'm sorry. I can't stay here anymore."

"I'm going to strangle my brother," CC said, tucking her blond-streaked dark hair behind her ear, green eyes flashing.

"Could someone please drive me into town?"

"Don't tell me he's going to screw up another good one," CC continued on with her anger.

She meant the last woman he'd loved. Chloe felt stabbing pain go through her heart.

"Don't worry," Bevy said. "He'll snap out of it."

"Yeah. You're not like the other women," CC said. "You're someone he can trust. Everyone can see that about you, Chloe. You're the genuine article. The real deal. You don't play games. You don't lie. You say it the way it is. He's got to know that. He's just scared."

"I should have known better."

Bevy clearly didn't like hearing that. "No, *he* should know better. Everyone can see that the two of you are getting close. CC's right, he's just scared. Give him some time, Chloe."

"I won't be with someone who judges me based on past experiences. He has to see me for who I am."

"He does. He will."

He turned away from her this morning like she was practically invisible. Nothing about last night had mattered, least of all her feelings. She wasn't going to forgive him for that.

"I wish I could stay, really. I love all of you. This Christmas was the best I've ever had. But Mason can barely look at me, and I can't stand to be treated that way. Please." She looked from Bevy's unreadable face to CC. "Will you drive me to town? I'll find a place to stay there."

"You can stay in the guesthouse," Bevy said, one last attempt to sway her.

That was so sweet. Chloe shook her head. "No. I don't want to be anywhere near him. Please. Try and understand."

"I understand that after I strangle him, I'm going to give my brother a black eye." CC stood and folded her arms. "He's such an idiot!"

Deirdra entered the kitchen and stopped behind Bevy. "I just came in from the woodshed. The guys are giving Mason hell out there, but he isn't budging."

Bevy stood from the table. "Take Chloe to town, CC. I'll give Mason the black eye."

Mason entered the house, his dad and Teddy right behind him, and stomped his feet. He looked for Chloe. Not seeing her, he was relieved. Last night had him so bogged down he could barely pay attention to anything his dad or Teddy said. Until they'd started grilling him about her. And then Deirdra had overheard and glared at him before turning to go back into the house. His whole family was ganging up on him. They loved Chloe. Already.

That only made the turmoil inside him worse. Yesterday, the whole day, and last night had been so perfect. He could fall in love with her. That thought had come to him after they'd gone to bed together. And it's what drove him out of her bedroom. He was so tangled up over her that he had to get away. Run. Chloe knew that. The way she'd looked at him this morning told him. It had also hit him with guilt. His turning away had hurt her.

Every time he thought about talking to her, he recoiled. Talking to her might lead to more of what had occurred and that was already too much. Best if he ended it now, before things really got out of control. Before she wrapped her heart around his and then left when he least expected it. Maybe if they hadn't slept together so soon he wouldn't feel like this. It was happening too fast. Relationships like that never lasted, and he didn't want a relationship. This had gone as far as he was willing to go.

Hanging up his jacket, he moved into the living room. His mom stood there with Deirdra, her arms folded and her face in an angry frown. Deirdra just looked smug. Like she was saying, *You're in for it now.*

His dad and Teddy hung up their jackets and stood beside him.

"What's this all about?" his dad asked.

Mason looked again for Chloe.

"She's gone," his mom said.

"Who?" Teddy asked, but Mason could tell he had a good enough idea. It was more disbelief that made him ask.

Disbelief that mirrored his own. "Where'd she go?"

"Away from you," Deirdra said.

Fear that had nothing to do with his heart flared into a raging flame. "What? Where is she?" He put his jacket back on. "You let her go?"

"She didn't want to spend another second around you," his mom said. He couldn't remember the last time he'd seen her so upset. "You bring a nice girl into this home and then you dare to treat her with anything but respect? I'm ashamed of you."

That pierced him. "Mom. There's a criminal on the loose who saw her with me."

Deirdra gasped and his mother's face paled.

"Forget about that." As angry as his mother had been, she'd gotten careless. "Where is she?"

"CC took her into town. I told her to take her to the apartment above Hank's."

Mason didn't wait. He dug into his coat pocket for the rental keys.

"I'll go with you," Teddy said.

"So will I." His dad followed.

Teddy he'd take, his dad, no. Mason stopped him with a hand on his chest. "You stay here with the girls." If anything happened, there'd be someone here to protect them. At least, that's what he wanted his dad to think. The truth was, Teddy knew what he was doing. His dad didn't.

Karl nodded. "Good thinking."

"We'll call you as soon as we find her and CC."

"How much is this going to cost?" Chloe spun in a circle inside the cute two-bedroom apartment. Two bedrooms! And it was furnished like a cottage and a dream.

"Rent's paid through the end of March," The balding owner of the gift shop downstairs said. "Last tenant had to move in a hurry. You pay a five-hundred-dollar deposit and the utilities and we'll call it square. After that, we'll talk."

Chloe glanced over at CC with a big smile.

"Looks like everything but Mason is going your way."

With the mention of Mason, Chloe's cheer fell flat. Hank handed her a key and she gave him cash. She'd need to find a bank to deposit her severance check.

"Bevy said you're good with greeting cards."

"Yes. I'm looking for a place to sell them."

"I'll give you a few names. The distributor I work with will be able to help you."

"Thank you." That was what she'd been missing in Chicago. Connections.

Hank left and Chloe put her luggage on the bed in the master bedroom. When she came back out, CC had her car keys in her hand.

"I better get back. Mason's probably blown a gasket by now."

"Hmm." Good. He needed a few gaskets blown.

A series of thumps interrupted them. Chloe went to the door and opened it, peering down the stairs that led both outside the back of the shop and into the shop itself. Hank lay at the bottom. Too late, she saw a man standing adjacent to the door at the top. His shaved head gave her a jolt of recognition. His eerie gray eyes sent her into fight mode. Axel. Leaping in front of the doorway, he kicked the door and shoved her, sending her falling backward.

CC screamed.

Axel tackled Chloe before she could position herself to fight. Then something hard hurt the side of her head.

"Get up."

Staring up into pale gray eyes, Chloe nodded. His dark, thin mustache looked drawn on.

While pointing the gun at her, he said to CC, "Move and your friend is dead."

Her frantic breaths revealed her panicked state. Chloe

wished she wouldn't give this dirtbag that much power. When the time was right, they'd fight back.

Axel wanted Mason, not her and CC. He wouldn't do anything too terrible until he lured his enemy. She tried to communicate something to that effect to CC, but CC was too frightened right now.

"Both you girls are going to go down those stairs and out the back door. I got a car out there. You'll get in, and you…" He jabbed Chloe's forehead with the gun. "You're going to drive."

"Just take me. Leave her," Chloe said. "You don't need her."

"Shut up. Move."

"You don't need her. I'll go, but leave her."

Drawing back the gun, he hit her temple. CC screamed again while Chloe tripped and corrected her balance. She debated whether to fight him then. He swung his aim to CC and that stopped her.

"Scream again and I'll shut you up for good," Axel said. "Now go out the door ahead of us."

Trembling, CC backed away instead.

"Now!"

She looked terrified as she sought Chloe's eyes.

"It's okay, CC," Chloe said. "Do what he says."

Stumbling, CC went through the door. Chloe followed with Axel changing the position of his gun to her kidney.

Down the stairs, CC whimpered as she stepped over Hank's body. Chloe saw his chest moving so she knew he was still alive. His hair was bloody, though, so he must have a head injury.

Outside, she searched for anyone who might be able to help them. The back alley was empty and likely sparsely traveled in this small town. She could see the street from here but no cars passed. It was cold. Neither she nor CC had their jackets. They were still up in the apartment.

Axel released her to grab CC. CC screamed again. "I said shut up. You hear me?"

"Please don't hurt us," CC pleaded.

"Drive," he ordered Chloe. She hurried to the driver's side of the dark gray sedan and got in while he shoved CC in the back. She whimpered again with fear when Axel slid in beside her, putting the gun to her head.

"Please let us go. Please."

"It's okay, CC," Chloe repeated. They had a better chance if they were both calm. She met CC's eyes through the rearview mirror and tried to reassure her silently.

"Drive north out of town. I'll tell you when to stop."

Chloe watched her surroundings. Cars passed the other direction but no one noticed them. People walked along the sidewalk on both sides of the street. A man saw them and looked as they passed. Did he see the gun against CC's head?

Moments later they were driving on a desolate road, thick forest on either side.

"What are you going to do?" Chloe asked.

"What I shoulda done the minute I first met your boyfriend. It would have saved me a lot of trouble."

"What good will it do to kill us?" He hadn't said he'd kill them, but he hadn't answered her question, either.

"You're going to bring him to me."

So, he'd use them as bait and once he had Mason, kill them all. She wouldn't tell him he'd be outnumbered. CC's brother would surely join Mason, and Chloe wasn't about to stand around and let them do all the work. She planned on making it out of this alive.

"Up here on the right, turn."

Chloe saw the turn. If it weren't for CC, she'd drive the sedan into a tree or something. Anything to put Axel off-balance long enough to take his gun.

"Don't do it, Chloe," CC said.

Chloe turned. Now wasn't the time to fight back. She drove up a narrow road that wasn't plowed, but there were tracks. Tracks that Axel had made. A small cabin came into view. She stopped where the road dead-ended in front of the small structure. Another vehicle was parked there.

"Open the door and get out."

CC opened the door and Axel forced her toward the cabin. Chloe followed, trying to figure out what to do. If he tied them they were finished.

Axel wore a black leather jacket and thin gloves. The jacket would slow him down. Despite the cold, Chloe was glad she wasn't wearing her own jacket.

Pushing the door open, Axel shoved CC hard as she stumbled into the cabin. She tripped and fell against another man wearing a black ski jacket and no gloves. He was slightly bigger than Axel and had light brown hair that came to his shoulders. His brown eyes were shrewd. Patient. Axel started to turn on Chloe. His gun was no longer on CC and the other man was busy helping her correct her balance.

Chloe jumped up and swung herself nearly horizontal for a roll kick. The element of surprise always worked for her. No one expected a girl to move like this. She wacked the gun from Axel's hand with one foot and rammed the heel of her boot right into his mouth before her roll was complete. Landing like Catwoman with her hands ready, she picked up the gun as Axel sprawled facedown on the floor.

He started to roll onto his back. Chloe straightened and kicked him to let him know she was watching. "Don't move or I'll shoot."

Looking up at the other man, she demanded, "Let her go or he's dead." Now he had his gun pressed against CC's head. Her eyes were wide but not as afraid after seeing Chloe fight.

When the man didn't do as she asked, Chloe knelt next to Axel and jabbed the gun against his head, satisfied with his grunt of pain. "Do it or I'll kill him."

The man shoved CC and she tripped toward the still open door, leaning against the frame and waiting there for Chloe.

"Now drop your gun," she told the man.

He hesitated.

"I'm not kidding around. I'll kill him."

"Drop your damn gun!" Axel yelled.

The man did.

Chloe picked it up and stood, aiming each weapon at each man as she backed toward the door. Axel rolled onto his rear and elbows, watching her with a little incredulity.

"Who are you?" Chloe asked the other man.

He cocked his head at her mockingly.

She decided not to waste time forcing him. "CC, go to the car."

Hearing CC's running feet, she continued to back through the doorway, and then running after her, keeping watch on the doorway. She could see Axel emerging. At the car, she shot the second vehicle's front and back tires on the passenger side before getting behind the wheel. With CC already in the seat next to her, Chloe put the guns on her lap and started the car. She saw Axel walking out of the cabin with a gun raised.

"Stay down!" She spun the sedan around as bullets hit the exterior. He must be aiming for the tires, copying her tactic. She should have checked them for spare weapons.

Driving too fast down the narrow, icy road, the tires slipped and she skidded. The rear end hit a tree and then the front sailed into another. She tried backing up. The tires spun.

"Damn it!" She twisted to look behind her.

Axel and the other man were walking toward them.

Chloe opened the door and fired both of the guns she had. The men ducked out of sight.

"Run through the trees!"

"What?"

"We're stuck and they'll kill us if we stay here. Now run!"

"Chloe!"

"CC, don't think. Just do what I tell you. Run through the trees. Head for the road. Do it!"

CC ran. Chloe ran behind her, looking back to make sure Axel and the other man weren't in sight.

"Which way?"

"A little more to the right. The road is that way." She pointed. CC had been too scared to notice details, but Chloe was no stranger to dangerous surroundings. Or dangerous people.

Another check behind them and Chloe spotted Axel. Where was the other man? "Keep running!"

She stopped behind the cover of a tree and tucked one gun in the front of her pants. Then, inching out from behind the tree, aimed the second gun. Fired. Bark from the tree inches from Axel's head sprayed. She heard him curse.

"That's right, dirtbag," she yelled, "I'm a good shot!"

Firing some more, she ran out of bullets. Tossing that gun to the ground, she turned and ran, weaving in and out of trees and glancing back several times. She didn't see him. But he was there. He'd just be more careful now. Searching around for the other man and not seeing him, Chloe ran faster.

Mason screeched to a stop in front of Hank's Gift Shop. Teddy alighted from the Yukon with him and they entered the store. No one was there. Not even customers. Mason led the way to the back. No one. At the back door, he exchanged looks with Teddy and the two drew their weapons. Mason opened the door.

Hank lay there in the open space of a back entry.

Teddy already had his cell phone out while Mason checked for breathing. Hank groaned. His eyes blinked open.

"Hank?"

"Man…hit me."

"I know, just stay still. Help is on the way."

Mason looked up the stairs and saw an open door. Sick with dread, he took the stairs three at a time. Inside, he saw CC's purse and then Chloe's. Both girls were gone.

Axel had taken them. Fury roared into a forest fire inside him. His sister. Chloe…

He fought for control. After this morning…

A siren grew louder as he rejoined Teddy in the area at the bottom of the stairs. Teddy still had his phone to his ear and had crouched beside Hank.

"I'm fine," Hank said grumpily.

The sheriff's car came into view and stopped near the entrance. That was fast. Mason looked down at Teddy, who shrugged. Straightening from Hank, he moved to stand beside Mason just outside the door.

Sheriff Murphy got out of his car. "One of you two call in a man with a gun?" He saw Hank and alarm changed his expression.

"I said I'm fine, damn it!" Hank roared, rubbing his head.

Just then a man came running toward them from the street. "Sheriff!"

Teddy spoke into his phone and ended his call, turning expectantly toward the man.

Breathless, the man came to a stop before them. "I saw someone holding a gun to a woman's head in a dark gray Impala. Another woman was driving." After he caught his breath he described all the people in the car.

Chloe.

"Which way were they headed?" Mason demanded.

"North."

North, out of town.

"There's only two roads between here and the ranch," Teddy said, keeping track with Mason's thoughts. "The first one leads to a cabin," he added.

"No one goes there anymore. Mom said it's falling apart," Mason said.

They both knew this area well. Axel wouldn't want to go very far. If he spent any time scoping the area, it wouldn't have taken long to discover the cabin, a gem to a criminal mind like his. Did he intend to use the women as bait to lure Mason with the threat of their lives?

"Let's get going," Teddy jarred him from thought.

More than ready, Mason turned and would have started for the Yukon along with him.

"You two should really let me handle this."

He faced the sheriff with Teddy.

"Now, I know you're an agent, Mason, and you, Teddy, a detective, but this here is my jurisdiction."

"You're not really going to play that card with us, are you?" Teddy asked in exasperation.

"What about Hank?" Mason used a more diplomatic approach. "He needs help getting to the clinic." The only one in town, a one-doctor outfit with a couple of paramedics and a nurse practitioner.

"I told you I'm fine!" Hank struggled to rise to his feet but slumped back down, his back bumping against the door frame.

Sheriff Murphy knelt beside him. "Don't move, Hank. We need to get you checked out."

"You stay with Hank," Teddy said.

"We'll brief you when it's over." Mason turned once again and this time didn't stop until he reached the Yukon.

When Teddy shut the passenger door after him, Mason drove fast out of the cramped parking area, fishtailing on snow and ice as he turned onto Main Street. Less than two minutes later, he reached the first turn. Slowing, he could see tracks but stopped so he and Teddy could check them.

"Fresh," Teddy said.

"Yeah." Good sign.

Mason pulled out his gun the same time Teddy did. Both men scanned the trees and listened. Nothing.

And then…gunfire.

With fear climbing up into his throat, he got back into the Yukon with Teddy and drove up the road. And then stopped.

"We better go on foot," Mason said.

"Yeah."

The sound of snapping branches brought them both to a standstill. Mason heard breathing.

"I see something!" a woman shouted.

"CC!" Teddy yelled.

"Teddy? It's Teddy."

Emerging from the thick forest of trees, CC ran to them. Mason searched for Chloe but didn't see her.

"Where's Chloe?"

CC threw herself into Teddy's arms, breathing crazily. "Oh, my God. He's after us. We have to get out of here!"

"CC. Where's Chloe?"

Stepping away from her brother, she turned and looked behind her into the trees. "She was right behind me."

A tremble shook his hands. He felt faint with dread. Not Chloe. The gunshot…

"Stay here with her," Mason demanded.

Running through the trees, he found CC's footprints and followed them. The deep snow made his progress slow. Movement ahead caught his eye. Not Chloe. He stopped and hid behind a tree, peering out. He searched the shadowy trees. Chloe's. She was on the ground.

"No." He couldn't lose her like this.

He started running again, keeping his gun lifted. When he reached her, he saw that she'd hit her head on a rock. But what had made her fall?

A gunshot rang out. Mason moved between Chloe and the gunman and scanned the trees for Axel. His head popped out from behind a tree, gun raised. Mason fired. Bark from the tree hit Axel's face. He could tell by the way his head flinched. Mason fired again, and again.

Axel turned and ran. Mason fired three more times,

until he could no longer see his targets retreating back. Another movement swung his aim. He didn't see anything. Had he imagined the movement? Searching further, he saw nothing. Only falling snow and the sound of wide open space. The urgency of Chloe made him abandon the instinct to chase.

Tucking his gun into the back of his pants, he bent over her. "Chloe." He felt her warm breath and breathed a sigh of heavy relief. Probing her head, he found her injury. No major laceration, but she could have fractured her skull.

"Chloe." He held her face in his hands, looking at her closed eyes, willing her to wake up. "Chloe."

He began checking for other injuries. He found a gun tucked in the waist of her pants. Taking it out, he looked at her face in wonderment and then set it aside to finish checking her. He made his way down her body and found bloody snow under one of her legs. The cause of her fall. Gunshot wound in her leg. Ripping her jeans where the bullet had torn through the material, he wiped away the blood so he could see the wound. The bullet hadn't penetrated. Only grazed her.

He bent his head, shaking off his fear. She wasn't critical. He didn't want to move her, but waiting for emergency services out here would be dangerous with Axel still on the loose. And it was too cold. He had to get her to the clinic in town. Lifting her, he turned and saw Teddy running toward them with his weapon raised.

"It's clear," he told him.

Teddy lowered his gun. "Is she okay?"

"She needs a doctor." He told him what he'd found on her.

Being knocked out like this scared him. He tried not

to jostle her and held her head as steady as he could as he made his way back to the Yukon.

The big SUV came into view. CC jumped out and raced toward them. "Oh, my God. Chloe! Is she okay?" She panted a few scared breaths. "This is all my fault."

Teddy grabbed her by her arm and led her back toward the SUV. "Get in, CC. We have to hurry."

He opened the front passenger side and she got in. Mason carefully took Chloe to the backseat and climbed in with her. Teddy turned the SUV around and headed back into town. Mason searched for Axel. Nothing.

He looked down at Chloe's beautiful face and last night's feverish loss of control gripped him. If he never got a chance to tell her what it meant to him, he'd live with a weighty regret, and yet the thought of facing that gave him a cold chill of dread.

"She was trying to protect me," CC said, beginning to cry.

"She'll be all right," Mason said, but he had no way of knowing that for sure until she had medical help. He'd take care of her. He'd make sure she was okay. And then what? He didn't want to think about anything beyond getting her better.

"She told me to run and she stayed behind to shoot at Axel."

Mason looked up at CC and down again at Chloe. Had she? She'd had a gun tucked in her pants. He supposed he shouldn't be surprised she knew how to shoot guns. He'd just never met anyone like her before.

Teddy was on his cell talking to the local doctor, arranging to meet at the clinic. It was too far to Great Falls. If necessary, Chloe could be transported from the clinic.

"Where did she get the gun?" Mason asked CC.

"She kicked Axel and took his. You should have seen her. The way she moved! It was like watching a movie."

So she'd learned how to fight, too. That shouldn't have surprised him, either, given where she came from. He felt a surge of pride and gladness. She'd kept a clear enough head to save herself and CC.

"She held the gun to Axel's head and made the other man let me go. And then she made him give her his gun. She took both of their guns! It was amazing. We'd have been dead if it hadn't been for her." CC faced forward in the passenger seat. "Or I would have been."

That bit of news alerted Mason. "What other man?" Chloe had forced guns from two men?

CC looked over her shoulder. "There was another man waiting at the cabin."

"Who was he?"

"I don't know. He never said his name and neither did Axel."

"What did he look like?"

He watched his sister try to remember and realized she'd been too frightened to register much. "Tall…I think. Brown hair…everything happened so fast, I…"

Chloe began to stir. He looked down and saw her eyes flutter open. The stunning blue of them pierced his armor. The intimacy they'd shared was a living thing between them, arresting his heart.

"Chloe?"

She met his gaze with eyes still out of focus. "Mason?"

She knew his name. Another good sign. "Yes." She tried to sit up but he stopped her. "Stay still."

"What happened?"

"Do you remember falling?"

"No." She seemed to struggle remembering. "The last thing I remember is running from Axel."

Teddy pulled the car to a stop in front of the clinic. The doctor and the nurse practitioner emerged with a stretcher. Mason helped get her onto it, following them inside and watching them take her into a room. Inside the small waiting area, he took out his cell and called his SAC.

"Mason." Reid answered. "Is everything all right? We still haven't found Axel. With Christmas and all…"

"Axel is here."

"In Montana?"

"Yeah. And he's got company."

The long silence spoke for his boss. "Who?"

"That's what I'd like to know."

"How did he find you?"

He explained what he and Chloe had already talked about when they'd seen Axel during the sleigh ride. Tanner had talked.

"Then we have to assume Donovan knew who you were," Reid said.

"Yeah, and if he did, why question me when I arrived at the party? Why wait for Axel?"

"Who never showed."

"Exactly."

"You think he never told Donovan who you were?"

"It's crossed my mind."

"Why would he do that?"

"To take over his operation. Start fresh in Chicago with no competition."

"With the FBI on to him? Doubtful."

"Unless he had help. Partnered up with someone not associated with Donovan. There was a man with him at the cabin."

"I see where you're going with this. I'm going to send some people your way. They'll be watching but out of sight. Don't say anything to your family. Let's keep it quiet and get this wrapped up in time for the New Year."

"I'd like that." Mason spotted the nurse heading toward them. He'd also like good news about Chloe.

Mason disconnected just as the nurse stopped before CC and Teddy. He walked over to them.

"It looks like she dodged the bullet, as it were," the nurse began. "No sign of a skull fracture, but you might want to take her to Great Falls for tests. We don't have those services here. Otherwise, I'd suggest making sure she rests over the next couple of days as long as you don't notice any worsening in her condition. Things like nausea, signs of lethargy or confusion, that sort of thing. No lifting or strenuous exertion. She needs rest."

"That won't be a problem." His mother would insist on pampering her.

"I bandaged up the cut on her thigh," the nurse said. "That will heal fine. Sheriff will want to question her. I had to report the gunshot wound."

Mason nodded. "When can she go home?"

"We're bringing her out now."

Mason was so caught up in how it felt to say *home* that he barely registered what the nurse said. He'd rather just let her go back to the apartment she'd rented from Hank, but that was out of the question until Axel was caught. The idea of taking her home felt too right for his already spinning confusion. Home was exactly where he wanted her. But he was afraid once she was there, he'd never want her to leave. And then he'd really be in trouble. Again.

Chapter 7

Chloe hadn't been happy to discover Mason brought her back to his parents' house. More than the pain in her head and leg had kept her up all night. Sometime during the early morning hours, she'd finally fallen asleep, and now it was after seven at night. Showered and dressed, she reluctantly limped her way down the stairs. She wasn't looking forward to facing him. CC, too, who for some absurd reason felt responsible for her injuries.

The house was quiet, and Chloe relaxed when she discovered no one was in the kitchen. While her stomach growled, she sneaked leftover tater tots and hot dogs from the kids from the refrigerator.

"You're up!"

She jumped and turned to see Bevy rush into the kitchen, her dark hair bobbing and her borderline plump form in jeans and a blue, green and red knit sweater.

"Go sit down. I'll get this for you." She took the

containers Chloe held and reached for a plate. "Hot dogs?"

"I'm fine, really. I can do it." She'd already doted on her enough. "I love hot dogs."

"Sit." Bevy pointed to the kitchen island. "Hot dogs it is, then." She shook her head in marvel.

Knowing it was useless to argue, Chloe went to a stool and sat. "Where is everyone?" Mason, especially, so she could avoid him.

Bevy heated the tater tots and hot dogs in the microwave. "Mason and Teddy are out doing another patrol around the house. Karl's upstairs checking the windows. Deirdra is down in the rec room with the kids. CC was—"

"I'm right here." She appeared in the kitchen, sitting next to Chloe. "How are you? Are you all right?" She surveyed Chloe.

"I'm fine," she repeated, feeling the two women's overdone concern. There was a good measure of guilt in there, too.

"How does your head feel? Does it still hurt? Maybe you shouldn't be up yet."

"I'm fine," she said with more force.

"But you—"

"Really, I'm fine."

Bevy set the plate of food in front of her. The hot dog was just as juicy with ketchup and relish as she loved. She looked from one anguished face to the other. "You both did nothing wrong, all right? If anything, Mason is to blame since he's the one who brought all this here. Me included."

That only marginally pacified both women.

"I panicked," CC said. "If I'd have kept my head you wouldn't have been shot."

"And I should have never let you out of this house," Bevy chimed in.

Moved by how much they cared, Chloe had to fight a wave of affection. "I would have fought those men regardless of what you did, CC, and Bevy, there's nothing you could have done to keep me here."

After a few seconds, Bevy's face eased with understanding. "You're a strong woman. The strongest of any Mason's brought home. I knew that about you from the start. I just didn't see it until now."

"Mason didn't, either," CC added. "You should have seen him when I told him what you did."

Mason was only glad she'd kept his sister from being hurt. Other than protecting her from Axel, he didn't care about her.

"Where did you learn to fight like that?" Bevy asked.

Chloe didn't want to talk about it. Learning self-defense had been a necessity. "I took some classes." From a thirty-year-old gang member who lived next door to her until he was arrested for murder. She picked up a tater tot, dipped it in ketchup and ate.

"It was amazing," CC said.

To Chloe, fighting wasn't a source of pride. Someone entering the kitchen saved her from further hero worship. But that someone was Mason. Seeing him made her heart flutter with excitement that she didn't want. He stopped short when he saw her.

"You two could use some privacy." Bevy moved around the island counter.

"No, it's okay," Mason said. "I'll just…go back outside."

"Oh, stop it, Mason, you're acting like a sixteen-year-old."

He appeared stunned as his mother ushered CC out

of the kitchen. And then he stood there staring at her as if he didn't know what to do.

Deciding to save him—and her—any more discomfort, Chloe abandoned her hot dog and stood from the stool. Intending to march past him, she was taken aback when he stopped her with his hand on her arm.

Reluctantly, she looked up at him. He still seemed rigid, but in his eyes she saw confusion, which only made it worse.

"Let go."

"Chloe…"

"I get it, okay? You made a mistake. But let me reassure you, it wasn't as big as the one I made letting it happen."

That made him pull his head back in bemusement. Hadn't he considered how she'd feel? She fumed.

"It's not…"

"Let go of me, Mason."

Heeding her stern tone, he let her go. Uncertainty all but radiated from him. Chloe didn't like how that made her speculate if he felt more than she thought. She had to get some fresh air. Clear her head.

Mason stood in the kitchen for several minutes, wracked with the same terrible sense of disorder that had afflicted him after he made love with Chloe. Only now it was worse. She sounded like him. She sounded like she was the one being left in the cold. And wasn't that exactly what he'd done? Funny, how he'd endeavored to avoid getting hurt again and he was the one doing the hurting now.

His mother was right. He was acting like a sixteen-year-old.

Christmas night had thrown him so off-kilter that

he hadn't been able to face Chloe. He'd discovered that nothing made him feel like running more than a woman he wanted to go the distance with.

Walking to the front door, he debated whether he should go after her. What would he say to her? What did he want to say? That they were finished? *No.* Can they just be friends?

No.

This Christmas was the best he'd ever had. Christmas night was one he'd never forget. He wanted to be with the woman who made it that way. He didn't want to stop seeing her.

Slipping on his jacket, he saw her heading along the path that led around the house to the stable. He'd just finished a patrol of the property with Teddy, but it was dark and anything could happen. She stopped in front of the stable door just as he'd anticipated. Unlatching the double doors, she opened one just enough to enter, pausing to look behind her.

Mason ducked behind a pine tree, happy she was at least practicing a little precaution. She'd already proven she could defend herself. When she disappeared inside the stable, he jogged to the door and pushed it open enough to see inside.

She stood before one of the Clydesdales, petting its cheek and gazing up at its huge head. Then she let her forehead fall against its nose. The Clydesdale nickered but didn't protest.

Mason heard her sigh.

"Mason talked a lot about this place."

Mason looked toward the far end of the stable along with Chloe. A man emerged from the shadows. He knew that voice. The man came farther into the light, wearing snow pants and a heavy jacket and winter boots. But his shaggy brown hair and eyes were familiar. Shock rendered him still.

Tanner?

His partner. His ex-girlfriend's husband...

"You." Chloe murmured her surprise, doing a fine job of hiding her fear, if she was afraid. Maybe she wasn't. He was going to have to get used to that. And then what she'd said registered.

Was Tanner the second man who'd been with Axel? How could it be?

Mason drew his gun and entered the stable. "Stay away from her."

Tanner stopped when he saw Mason's weapon. "I should have known you wouldn't be far behind." He glanced over at Chloe. "A fine woman like that under the same roof would make me follow her around, too."

Missing pieces poured through Mason's mind. Axel's suspicion had always bothered him. Except it hadn't been suspicion, it had been knowledge. And it was that knowledge that had kept him away from Donovan's party. Donovan hadn't known who Mason was. Axel had. Tanner had told him everything and had warned him the raid would probably be moved up. Maybe he and Tanner had planned it that way. To get rid of Donovan.

"Was it convenient for you to have the FBI raid Donovan's party?" he asked Tanner.

"I haven't flipped sides, if that's what you're implying."

"No? Chloe, go back into the house."

She sidled her way over to him and stopped. "I'm staying with you."

She had to know he didn't have time to argue with her. And she was a fighter.

"I got close to Axel. So close that he told me what he wanted to do."

"Take down Donovan and anyone who followed him so he could run his own prostitution operation? Run it under a false name?"

"You were always quick."

Mason shook his head. "Why? Why throw away a legitimate career for…Axel?"

"I told you, I haven't flipped sides."

"You really expect anyone to believe you faked your own death for the sake of the investigation? Without telling anyone? You know the rules. That's one you don't break."

Tanner seemed to realize his tactic wasn't going to work. "I don't have rich parents, Mason. I have to live off what the government pays me, and that isn't enough."

"Does your wife know what you've done?"

Tanner's face hardened and he said nothing. Mason also sensed Chloe looking at him. Was she alarmed that he'd asked such a question? Or had she just realized Tanner was his partner?

He couldn't stop to explain. He had to know what had driven Tanner to this extreme. How could he leave a beautiful wife for a life of emptiness and crime? "I wonder how she felt when they showed up to tell her you were dead?"

"She probably celebrated," Tanner sneered.

Mason began to get a bad feeling about this. There was more that drove Tanner than making money illegally.

"Oh, come on, Mason. Don't play it like you didn't know. It was always you she wanted, not me."

Chloe's head turned toward him again.

He couldn't reassure her now. "We were finished a year before you started seeing her. She might have loved me once but she didn't when she met you."

Tanner grunted a derisive laugh. "Being married to her made teaming up with Axel real easy. What did I have to lose? A lousy paying job and a wife who didn't love me? I can make a lot of money working with Axel. Like I said, it was an easy choice."

"Tanner. Think about what you're doing. You're making a mistake. You're basing your decisions on the belief that Renee still loves me."

"She does, Mason. She stayed away, but she does love you."

Mason shook his head, not buying it. "Is that why you're here? Did you and Axel have some kind of agreement to get me before you went into business together?"

Unmoved, Tanner said, "When we had sex on our honeymoon, it was your name she cried out, not mine. I started to hate her after that. You, too. Do you think I enjoyed working with you knowing my wife was probably thinking of you every time I slept with her?"

"You don't know that."

"She told me she still loved you. You, Mason. It killed me to hear it but I needed to know for sure before I started to work with Axel. I asked her and she said she got so tired of waiting for you to come around that she thought she'd fallen out of love with you. She said it wasn't until shortly before our wedding that she realized she was marrying the wrong man, and that the man she should have married was you."

Mason shook his head, confused and then…not. He looked over at Chloe. It had never been as good with any woman as it was with her. Renee was nice and beautiful but she'd turned her back on him. Granted, he may have deserved it, but she'd allowed too much time and pain to pass. It only made him doubt that she ever truly loved him. He wouldn't have known that if he'd never met Chloe. Renee didn't have her special qualities. He couldn't even name them all. The survivor in her defined a lot of who she was, but she also had professional drive. And heart. She had a pure, honest, loving heart, something he'd been craving without even knowing. Until now.

Realizing he was still looking at Chloe and she was as immersed in the exchange as much as him, he wanted to tell her. He wanted her to know how much last night meant. How much he wanted to keep seeing her.

Just as Mason began to turn his attention back to Tanner, the man drew his gun and moved quick in bringing the barrel against Chloe's forehead.

"Drop your gun, partner."

Chloe's mouth dropped open, caught as off guard as Mason.

"Think about what you're doing," Mason tried again. "It might not be too late to fix this. Give us Axel and work a deal. Don't go any further."

"It's already too late for that."

Mason's cell phone rang.

Tanner glanced down to Mason's jean pocket and then back up at him. "Don't answer it. There's only one person I came here for tonight, but the problem is, now we have a witness."

Chloe remained calm.

"If I kill you both, Axel will be blamed."

"I wouldn't be so sure about that," Mason said, keeping his gun on Tanner.

"I'm not the only one who saw you at that cabin," Chloe added. "CC will be able to describe you."

Mason didn't correct her and say she wouldn't.

"Then I guess my work isn't finished tonight." And then with more force, "Drop your gun."

What, he'd actually try to kill CC with Teddy and Mason's dad prepared for an attack? The deadly change in Tanner's eyes warned him that he was about to shoot Chloe. He glanced at her and read her readiness. Keeping his gun aimed at Tanner, he waited for her move. She began to crouch. Knocking Tanner's gun arm, he punched him. Chloe landed backward onto her hands, lifting her legs acrobatically and ramming the side of Tanner's knee with the uninjured one.

It was enough for Mason to block Tanner's swinging aim and grab hold of his wrist to keep him from shooting anything living. Shoving his pistol under his chin, he felt Tanner go still.

Mason's phone rang again. This time Chloe slid her hand into his pocket and answered.

"This is Chloe Bradford. I'm in the stable with Agent Jaffee. His partner is in here with us and he has a gun!"

"Bitch!" Tanner spat.

Mason managed to pry Tanner's gun from his grip and hand it over to Chloe, who took it with her free hand and aimed for Tanner's chest.

"Yes. Tanner. He's alive." She paused. "Mason has him under control now." She paused again, this time longer. "Okay, I'll tell him." She disconnected and tucked his phone into her own jean pocket. "There are agents down at the end of the driveway," she explained. "They're on their way."

"Good."

She turned to him again. "You knew they were here?"

"Yes."

"Why didn't you tell us?"

"To keep it real for Axel…and Tanner," he added with disgust.

"They have Axel."

He shot her a quick look. "Where was he?"

"He was waiting for Tanner down on the road." She turned to Tanner. "Apparently, it wasn't his idea to come here and he's angry he's caught."

Tanner roared and lunged, charging like a bull into Mason. They fell to the ground together, Mason struggling to maintain control of his pistol.

Horses shuffled and whinnied nervously.

"Mason!" Chloe shouted.

Tanner was a madman with nothing to lose, clawing and punching wildly. Mason slammed his gun against his head. They wrestled. Breaking free, Mason rolled and jumped to his feet. Tanner was slower to stand. Mason punched him and moved behind him, hooking his arm around his neck. Tanner twisted away. Mason raised his gun, ready to fire.

Tanner hesitated.

The sudden bang of the stable doors opening preceded a swarm of four black-clad agents. "FBI! Don't move!"

They surrounded Tanner, who stared at Mason with crazed fury.

Chloe gave the gun she held to one of the agents. After flipping the safety on his pistol, Mason tucked it into the back waist of his jeans and went to Chloe. She slid her arm behind him as he curved his around her upper torso.

Tanner was cuffed and taken out of the stable. Mason followed, taking Chloe's hand. They walked along the pathway to the front of his parents' house. Everyone was outside. His mom and dad, CC, Deirdra and Teddy. The kids stood up on the porch in their pajamas, bundled in jackets and boots, huddled together by their older brother.

Axel sat in an unmarked car. Tanner was led to the other side and forced inside. Mason could see the two begin to argue.

Slipping an arm around Chloe, he would have walked with her toward the house, but she moved away, eyeing him warily before walking ahead of him.

With Axel and Tanner caught, there was no longer any danger standing in her way. She could leave tonight and go back to her new apartment. She could be out of his life for good if that was what she wanted…what she truly wanted.

Somehow, he had to make her want to keep seeing him. He wasn't running anymore.

Chapter 8

Chloe saw the way Mason was looking at her and moved to stand beside CC. Once again, everyone had gathered in Bevy and Karl's huge kitchen, where Bevy had busily prepared late night snacks and everyone had a glass of wine to relax and celebrate the resolution of an eventful night. Mason stood near the entryway underneath that damnable mistletoe. She could feel his desire to be alone with her and that scared her.

After the way he'd withdrawn the morning after Christmas night, she wasn't anxious to give in to hope just yet. They'd been under a lot of pressure with Axel on the loose. Things would be a lot different once they returned to normal. And normal for her was getting away from here and starting her new life in Woodland, Montana.

CC elbowed her. "Mason's under the mistletoe."

"I see that."

"I think he went there on purpose."

Chloe watched the way Mason answered something Teddy said and resumed staring at her. His eyes had a twinkle to them, as if he were smiling without it showing on his mouth.

"You kiss him, then," Chloe said.

CC sent her an incredulous look. "He's my brother."

"I'm not kissing him."

"I talked to him earlier. He said he was taking more time off from the FBI than he originally planned."

"Good for him."

"That means he'll be around awhile."

Not so good for her.

"Did you know Dad asked him if he was ready to start working the ranch?"

Chloe turned from Mason's intoxicating green eyes. "Why did he ask him that?"

Flipping her blond-streaked hair back over her shoulder, eyes twinkling with mischief, she smiled big. "Didn't think you knew that."

Was his entire family conspiring to get them together?

"He'll inherit the ranch when Mom and Dad die. Everybody's known for a long time that Teddy doesn't want to work it and neither do I. I wouldn't be any good at it."

"Good for him."

"I think dad asked him for a reason." She wiggled her eyebrows.

Not so good for her.

"Chloe, why don't you and Mason go bring more firewood in?" Bevy suggested, sugar-sweet.

A blunt *no* was on the tip of her tongue.

"I'll help Mason," Teddy said. "You girls stay in here where it's warm."

"Teddy, you will stay right where you are." Bevy gave him an obvious warning look.

Teddy glanced from her to Chloe and then to Mason. "Oh."

"Yeah, oh," CC mocked. "You idiot."

Teddy grinned. "Hey, I've been happily married for years. I forgot how much of a chess game dating can be." He went over to Deirdra and kissed her smiling mouth.

Chloe looked from one expectant gaze to the next, ending with Mason's triumphant one.

"I need to talk to you anyway," he said.

CC elbowed her again. "He needs to talk to you." She nudged her firm enough to make her take two steps toward Mason.

With the kitchen silent and all eyes on her, Chloe slowly approached him. He led her to the front entry.

"There's plenty of wood by the fireplace," Chloe pointed out.

Mason looked there and then back at her. "We'll just bring in a bundle," he said, and then lower, "just enough to satisfy the family."

Satisfy the family.

They'd be satisfied if she ended up with Mason. The idea kept her from reaching for her jacket.

"I'll carry the wood. You're still limping a little."

After putting on his jacket, Mason took hers off the rack and presented her with it open and ready for her arms.

Reluctantly, she slipped her arms into the sleeves and he adjusted it on her shoulders. She zipped it up and he handed her some gloves. She put those on and he pulled a hat down over her head. She was still wearing her hiking boots and so was he.

Outside, the chill made her long for a fire right now. She followed Mason to the woodshed. There, he turned to face her.

She bent to begin loading an armful. *Just get this over with.* Her leg was fine, she could carry a few sticks of wood. She'd endure the night and be alone in her own place in the morning. She'd start over. Fresh. New. It would rejuvenate her.

Mason stopped her with a hand on her shoulder. "Wait."

Abandoning the wood, she straightened and faced him. Seeing his face worked to undo her.

"I'm sorry I didn't stay with you on Christmas night," he said.

The all-out apology might be enough if she didn't know what had driven him away. "Don't worry about it."

"And the way I avoided you yesterday morning."

"It was a mistake. We let it happen too soon, that's all. No big deal."

"You don't understand."

"Don't I?"

"That night..."

Hearing his difficulty, Chloe wondered if he was only being nice because he'd saved her from Axel. It didn't change the way he felt about women, or didn't want to feel.

"I wasn't expecting it to happen, Chloe. And afterward, I wasn't prepared for the way I felt."

Chloe stiffened. Letting her heart go free over this was risky. They had a long road ahead of them if they decided to make a go of it. She'd never been afraid to end a relationship with a man she didn't trust, no matter how much she liked him. But she was afraid with Mason. He'd already shown her he could walk away. She wasn't ready to trust him. She couldn't invest all of herself for a man who'd only end up disappointing her later.

Somehow she had to make him understand that. "What are you saying? That you'll move to Montana to be with me?"

To his credit he didn't avert his gaze. "That is a logistical problem."

Meaning, he was still too injured from past experience to take that big of a leap. "I don't even know where you live."

"That's obvious."

She could tell he was fighting a grin. Shock and something too close to blind hope flared up in her. "You live here?"

"Well, no, not *here*. Missoula."

"You live in Missoula."

"We'd have to manage the long drive if we're going to start seeing each other."

Was he serious? Catching herself falling for more of that the hope, the survivor in her cut it short.

"You're off the hook, Mason. You don't have to do this."

"You know this is for real, Chloe."

Angling her head with all her doubt, she folded her arms.

"You know, and you're afraid."

"*I'm* afraid?"

"I was afraid, too. I'm not saying I wasn't. I was afraid of falling in love with someone who wasn't real, of not finding someone like that." He paused. "I have, Chloe. I found you."

Oh. That was so sweet. And deep down, she heard the truth of what he said.

"You're real," he continued with the torture. "You don't say things you don't mean. I know that if you're with me, you won't be with anyone else."

"Renee was faithful to you."

"Yes, she was, but that wasn't meant to be. This is. You and me. Don't you feel it?"

Yes, her heart cried out. Yes, she felt it. She felt it too much. What was beginning to brew to life between them was strong. Undeniable. Like nothing she'd ever experienced.

She looked toward the house. Losing the last family she'd gotten close to had shattered her. She couldn't bear to lose this one, too.

"Like me, they already love you," Mason said.

Chloe grunted to hide how much she needed to hear that. But she couldn't. She just couldn't take that step.

"I don't know, Mason. You've been through so much with women. And I…I've been through my own trouble. Maybe it's not such a good idea."

"Marry me, then. I'll prove to you how much you mean to me. How much I believe in this. In *us.*"

"Mason," she whispered, tingles of love and affection spreading all over her body. But it was so soon. Was he serious?

"We can pick a date sometime next year so we have time to date first," he said.

He wasn't going to give up on her. Even if she put him off now, she doubted he'd stop pursuing her. That touched her. She also thought his suggestion wasn't so off the mark. They'd be engaged while they dated. He'd do that. For her. She was worth that much to him.

All this time she'd thought he was the only one doing the running. But the only one doing the running right now…was her.

She was running from the risk of belonging to a family, only to have it ripped away, leaving her once again alone, as she had been since her senior year in high school.

"I'll go get you a ring tomorrow," Mason declared. "I'll do anything to keep seeing you, Chloe."

Yes! Instinctually, she knew she'd never stop wanting to be with him. What they had was an all-encompassing infatuation. Over time, it would grow into deep love. She felt it in her heart. And he felt it, too.

"Mason…" She stepped closer to him.

He put his gloved hand on the side of her face. "Marry me."

"Okay."

He searched her eyes. "Do you mean it?"

She nodded. "Yes. Oh, yes!" She could recognize his need not to wait this time. As soon as he saw that this was the real thing, he'd asked her to marry him. He wasn't doing it just to prove his love to her, or his belief in the love that would grow between them. He was asking because he'd been afraid to ask Renee to marry him, and this time he wasn't going to let the woman who mattered most to him go.

"Yes." She threw herself against him. Holding her close, he kissed her. She shivered, and not just from cold. "Let's get the wood and go inside."

"I'll get the wood."

She pushed him aside to make room for her at the woodpile. "I'm fine, Mason. I can carry some wood."

"Okay." He handed her three pieces. "Take those."

Letting him get away with that, she carried the split logs as he carried a full armful toward the house. Inside, a fire already crackled in the fireplace and no one was in sight. The kitchen was in a rare state of silence.

She exchanged a look with him.

"I guess it's obvious what they want."

"Us together." She was so thrilled about that.

He dumped his armful of wood onto the already burgeoning pile and helped her deposit her three pieces.

"Instead of staying here tonight, why don't we stay in the other house?"

The original house his grandfather had built. She hadn't seen the interior yet. She couldn't wait. Would they live there? What a dream.

Her smile must have given her away.

"We can live there if you want."

She nodded vigorously. "Yes! Yes!"

He chuckled. "Good. We'll wake up with each other in our new house and spend the day together. Drive into Great Falls to find you a ring. Then we'll spend New Year's Eve with the family tomorrow night."

The family. Her family. Their family.

Pure joy all but burst inside her. They'd see her ring tomorrow night. "Oh, Mason. Is this really happening?" She looped her arms around his shoulders and he loosely held her around her waist.

"Yes. And I couldn't be happier."

"Me, neither."

"Merry Christmas, Chloe." He kissed her.

"Happy New Year, Mason."

He kissed her again. "The best ever."

Clapping and cheers erupted.

Chloe moved back with Mason and turned to see his

entire family in the kitchen. They must have hidden out of sight when they'd entered. Now they all stood clustered in the wide entry of the kitchen.

Looking from one smiling face to the next, Chloe reveled in the sparkling joy that consumed her. This was her family now.

Mason took her hand with his.

"Leaving Chicago was the best decision I ever made."

"Bringing you here was mine."

When his family approached and surrounded them with heartfelt congratulations, she couldn't agree more.

* * * * *

SUSPENSE

Heartstopping stories of intrigue and mystery—
where true love always triumphs.

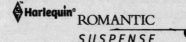

COMING NEXT MONTH
AVAILABLE NOVEMBER 22, 2011

#1683 A CAVANAUGH CHRISTMAS
Cavanaugh Justice
Marie Ferrarella

#1684 CAPTAIN'S CALL OF DUTY
The Kelley Legacy
Cindy Dees

#1685 COPPER LAKE SECRETS
Marilyn Pappano

#1686 MILLIONAIRE'S LAST STAND
Small-Town Scandals
Elle Kennedy

*Lucy Flemming and Ross Mitchell shared a magical,
sexy Christmas weekend together six years ago.
This Christmas, history may repeat itself when they find
themselves stranded in a major snowstorm...
and alone at last.*

Read on for a sneak peek from
IT HAPPENED ONE CHRISTMAS
by Leslie Kelly.

Available December 2011, only from Harlequin® Blaze™.

EYEING THE GRAY, THICK SKY through the expansive wall of
windows, Lucy began to pack up her photography gear.
The Christmas party was winding down, only a dozen or so
people remaining on this floor, which had been transformed
from cubicles and meeting rooms to a holiday funland. She
smiled at those nearest to her, then, seeing the glances at her
silly elf hat, she reached up to tug it off her head.

Before she could do it, however, she heard a voice. A
deep, male voice—smooth and sexy, and so not Santa's.

"I appreciate you filling in on such short notice. I've
heard you do a terrific job."

Lucy didn't turn around, letting her brain process what
she was hearing. Her whole body had stiffened, the hairs on
the back of her neck standing up, her skin tightening into
tiny goose bumps. Because that voice sounded so familiar.
Impossibly familiar.

It can't be.

"It sounds like the kids had a great time."

Unable to stop herself, Lucy began to turn around,
wondering if her ears—and all her other senses—were
deceiving her. After all, six years was a long time, the mind

could play tricks. What were the odds that she'd bump into *him*, here? And today of all days. December 23.

Six years exactly. Was that really possible?

One look—and the accompanying frantic thudding of her heart—and she knew her ears and brain were working just fine. Because it was *him*.

"Oh, my God," he whispered, shocked, frozen, staring as thoroughly as she was. "Lucy?"

She nodded slowly, not taking her eyes off him, wondering why the years had made him even more attractive than ever. It didn't seem fair. Not when she'd spent the past six years thinking he must have started losing that thick, golden-brown hair, or added a spare tire to that trim, muscular form.

No.

The man was gorgeous. Truly, without-a-doubt, mouth-wateringly handsome, every bit as hot as he'd been the first time she'd laid eyes on him. She'd been twenty-two, he one year older.

They'd shared an amazing holiday season.

And had never seen one another again.

Until now.

Find out what happens in
IT HAPPENED ONE CHRISTMAS
by Leslie Kelly.
Available December 2011, only from Harlequin® Blaze™

Harlequin®

ROMANTIC
SUSPENSE